California Roadkill²

The In Between

by
GenXCore

Foreword
by
James Remar

CALIFORNIA ROADKILL 2
by GenXCore

Published by Mystic Boxing Commission®
Attn: Publisher Daniel Yaryan
dyaryan@gmail.com
www.sparringartists.com

ISBN#: 979-8-9905623-9-4
1st Edition: October 2025 – Mystic Boxing Commision

This book is dedicated to my mother
For showing the way with patience and love,
Determination and grit.

FOREWORD

by

James Remar

The awe of pounding hollow surf. The joy of the hyper kinetic impossibly charming dudes and dudettes who challenge massive barrels of death with absolute joy and mania. The eerie timeless solitude of the SoCal coast with it's magnificence oddly urban isolation and untamed wilderness, The In Between so perfectly sets the stage for its unfolding you can almost taste the ocean salt and smell the surf-wax.

Our central observer is a truly "in between" kind of guy ...to surf or not to surf...he observes his friends with an obsessive detachment lest he get sucked back in and yet he relishes every moment of skirting danger with them.

Where his peers are wild in their abandon he is keeping "it together."

Sea Nymphs, Rock and Roll Punk musicians, ersatz gurus, and recovery are all in a tenuous balance that is at all times tempered with love.

The In Between is a beautiful kind of sober reality for our central voice. Overwhelmed and at the same time balancing above a jagged valley...his inner dialogue so generously shared with us...offers a real glimpse of the mind of one who has the gift of a sober life and the unrelenting reality of this gift.

Reading The In Between is like a great surf session...gotta paddle out for ONE MORE WAVE!

The In Between

"We are well advised to keep on nodding terms with the people we used to be, whether we find them attractive or not."

—Joan Didion

“The future’s uncertain and the end is always near.”

—Jim Morrison

Prologue

DEAR READER, traveler, sufferer, tormentor. This is for you. I know how you feel. I do. If you've made it this far, there are no platitudes, no consolation prizes. All I can really say is: You are, despite your experience, your proof of abandonment and abuse, not alone. If but for no one else I am here, in these pages, in my shit-fuck camper, just like you. Alone and hungry, angry and full of pity, want, and regret. I, too, am tired. I write because this is the only place we can find one another, The In Between. And because I know you know how it feels. Unheard and unseen, this is our bond. Within these pages we can find Love. And I know it's not much, Love; an ill-fitting bandage on an infected wound; an old dirty rubber band loosely wrapped around a broken and homeless bone. No money. No food. What the fuck? But I, like you, have nothing else to give. Our shared experience is all there is now. So come with me, a little further. See my mistakes.

If only not to feel,
So goddamn fucking
All alone.

Chapter One: Discordant

I HAD NO BUSINESS BEING in the water. My muscles were stiff and weak with years of underuse; my ears echoed loud with adrenaline and the sound of air filling my lungs. Sets of waves were coming in double overhead, fat and hollow. The break was alive and angry in its perfection, its Retribution, hence the name.

"Dig, motherfucker!" Donny said, looking back at me. "Dig!" He was strangely spry and buoyant on his board, grinning, a child at sea, unafraid, willingly rushing into whatever may come.

I struggled to catch my breath and make it through the pummel of the middle break; The In Between where waves held no form but that of a giant wall. Cold water rushed through the neck of the new Turley wetsuit I wore; chest to groin, down into the thighs, it was a chilled wake up call.

Rich had already made it to the outside break.

"Fuck it," Donny said.

He turned his board around and took off late on a massive closeout with nowhere to go but into the hollowed void. Why would someone do that? Fuck you, that's why.

Sometimes, you just gotta go.

I ducked under the wave that Donny took off on, absorbed its punch, pulled out the back, and quickly turned only to watch him emerge from the frothy tumult smiling wild like the teenager I had met all those years ago. *Maybe he was right, Lord.* Maybe all he really needed was this. Maybe it really was L.A. and the music and the talent and all the internal obligations that real talent entails. For him, a kind of limited vast. Maybe all of it meant nothing compared to the feeling, the exhilaration, of willingly going into a maxed-out, closeout barrel in The In Between at Retributions and emerging unscathed.

It was inspiring.

I decided to do the same.

The drop was steep and awkward due to my poor positioning and rust. To my surprise I pulled it off, and instead of going for the closeout I bottom turned hard and smashed the lip with an incredible amount of speed and force. It was almost as if I'd had luck on my side. On the way down, a figure appeared beneath me. I kicked off the board and fell into the churn. I popped up out of the water and could hear Donny yelling. What? I don't know. It was indecipherable. I immediately had to duck under another incoming wall of water.

I again emerged only to go back under again, a third time.

When I arose, I could see Donny sitting upright on his board, attempting to balance, in the swirling foam of white water. The figure was next to him. "Jimmy, look who it is!" he yelled.

I paddled closer. It was Hana. She was naked. Her body was firm, strong with proper form as she held the nose of her board with her left hand, and gently waded with her right, a pro in total control.

Donny splashed at her.

She splashed back.

Donny splashed at her again.

She splashed back again.

"Nice ass," he said.

Despite the movement in the water, she sat up on her boardperfectly balanced, thighs and waist submerged, foam up to the midriff. Her hair was long and full and thick, a salted blonde dread slicked back wet over the ears, her breasts, tan, firm, supple, erect, alive from the cold salt water. Minus a few lines and sun-induced freckles, she was, like her mother before her, a woman of Dover, of earth and ocean; a seemingly barely-aged beauty not only stuck in time, but naked and presumably on Seroquel.

"You shouldn't be here," she said curtly. "Either of you."

Donny shrugged as if to say, *Fuck you talking about*?

She turned to me. "What are you looking at?"

Her eyes were a piercing blue and made me uncomfortable—too much to see, too much information, a limitless window revealing everything and nothing at all.

"It's cold. What are you doing?"

"Surfing," she said coy, mocking. "What are you doing?"

"Hana, you're naked."

She shook her head in bemused contempt.

"No… Jimmy. You are."

"How about a pleasantry? Shit. 'How you been,' like that," Donny said.

"You steal my shit? Want me to be pleasant?"

"Ain't no one stealing no one's shit. Just got here."

She smirked and nodded up to the cliffs and Fairview, inferring an awareness, a watchful eye.

"Here to get rich, that it? Recovery rich."

"No one's here to get anything," I said. "The water's freezing. What are you doing?"

"Still straddling that line huh, Jimmy?" she said. She had seen everything she needed to see, and I had clearly not passed the test. "Wetsuits are for pussies." She waded her arms a few times for balance. "Not gonna get rich stealing backpacks. Only the rich get Rich around here. You should know that by now." She paused, then smirked. "Except Joy, maybe. Everyone else… slaves. That why you're here, Marsan? Marsanovic. Mr. Ideal. Get your Joy back?" She opened her arms. "Should've stuck with me. Be better off."

"Oh damn!" Donny said.

"Hana, what are you talking about? I just fucking—"

"I'm talking about that!" pointing forcefully to Fairview. "And that!" to the Compound. "And that!" to the Heights. "And that!" to the Turley wetsuit I wore and the Turley board I was floating on.

As she continued to point and spout incoherent, Rich took off on a monster set wave from the outside break. His take-off and bottom turn were an image of perfection, a long smooth line ahead of him, his world, his wave to do with as he pleased. Above him the sun burned a hole through the vaporous coastal eddy. Hana stopped her pointing. Donny turned. We watched Rich carve the face of the wave as if it were his canvas, he the painter with grace and power, complete awareness of the palette, and what the piece, the wave, would require. Behind him, more sets were coming in.

"Fuck yeah!" Donny said. He began to paddle out.

Hana leaned back on her board, the nose rising out of the water revealing a spray-painted rendering of the Turley 'T' inside the circle, along with a small pocketknife inside of a black Velcro strap. Apparently, she wasn't above free Turley merch herself. In a single motion she ripped on the Velcro, pulled out the knife, and thrust forward to catch

Donny and cut his leash. "Nice ass yourself," she said passing him by.

"Oh no you fucking didn't!"

"Suck on that, suck ass."

Donny forged ahead, a risky move in surf that big without a leash. Would be a long swim back to the shore. I trailed behind.

Rich kicked off the wave so as to not get stuck in The In Between. There was no reform on his wave and the three of us had to duck dive underneath the fast-approaching mountain of whitewash. I held onto the rails tightly, but it was of no use. The board immediately ripped out of my hands. I flailed in the wash, pummeled as if on a firing line of rubber pellet machine guns. The leash pulled hard on my leg. Down I went, losing my sense of direction. Instead of swimming up to the surface, I swam down to the silted sand bottom. Upside down, I didn't have the right balance or positioning to push up with my legs. I clawed furiously up, into and through the psychotic wash.

I reached the surface. The roar of the ocean and the churn of the whitewash was deafening. I gasped for air and promptly received a mouthful of salted foam. The outside break was now nothing but lines of incoming waves.

I was stuck in The In Between, the worst place to be. With little strength left, I realized I wasn't going to make it to the outside break. Not only that, I may not make it back to shore.

I looked for Donny. His board bobbed up and down in the wash and headed toward the trough. About twenty feet away, he popped out of the water and waved his hand in the air. I yanked on my leash, it was tight and extended, and got back on the board. I paddled to him. Nothing worse than swimming with your back against waves or whitewash that consistent, that big.

Not only is it dangerous but it feels like retreat, a loss.

When I reached him, I rolled off the board into the water so he could hold on and float. Out of breath, he couldn't speak but nodded to the next wave coming through: a thick and soon-to-be-hollow wall of water rising, this time a reform ready to unleash its power onto the ocean's surface. There was no way I could duck dive again with the board; didn't have the air to go back down again; and it would've pulled me too far away from Donny. I reached for my ankle, ripped off the leash and ditched the board. We were now both of us—perhaps as we always were—on our own; no tether, floating into the unknown.

The suck from the outgoing tide pulled us fast into the swelling rush of the wave. We went under.

And it was much easier; it always is when you let go. The wetsuits buoyant, we were able to use the push/pull force of the tide to go under the wave and quickly come out the backside. With a moment in between to tread water and catch our breath before the next wave came in, Donny said, "Not going to be able to do this forever!"

Breathing heavy, his eyes were wide open, clearly aware of the situation we were in. "Catch our breath... bodysurf the clean-up set, get us through the trough."

"You sure?"

He spit a mouthful of water. "Gonna be too far."

I nodded in agreement.

The trough is a deep pool near the shore that can, under the best of circumstances, be tough to swim through depending upon the tide, the time of year, upwelling. But with waves this size, the whitewash of a clean-up set can, if timed right, provide the needed push to make it through the trough and onto the shore.

"You see Hana?" I asked.

"No. She probably made it outside."

Another reform wave approached.

"Okay. Not this one, the next."

We again rode the strong pull of the outgoing tide into and under the wave. Out we came floating in the swirl, the momentary in between, weightless and waiting for the next outward suck. We said nothing and treaded, waiting for the clean-up set. It didn't take long. A massive milky spume, a dumpster of a wave, hostile, with no sign of blue or green.

"Here we go."

"You get turned upside down, get your arms, legs up."

"Just like old times," he grinned.

"Yeah. You ready?"

"Fuck yeah. Let's do this!"

Freestyle, we swam hard against the pull of the tide to get ahead of the wave and make the take-off without getting pulled up and over the falls. Down the face we went on our bellies. In my periphery, a dirty latherous tunnel howled as I prepared for an abuse the wave did not fail to deliver. Into the wash I went, a bowling ball in an industrialized washing machine. I rolled over and over and over again. Upside down, the moment came, and I stuck out my leg and used the force of the whitewash to propel me through the trough and onto the shore.

On my hands and knees, I crawled. The sand was coarse from the churn, composed mostly of broken shells. I looked for Donny but did not see him. I dragged myself up onto the sandbar. There he was.

"Need some lifeguards up in this bitch," he said.

Breathing like a fiend and somewhat embarrassed by it, I fell onto my back and stared up into a small patch of blue sky, a hole in between where the sun burned through the fog. A clearing. The surrounding resonance of Retributions—waves against waves against rocks against man—filled my ears with a silent void reminiscent of a well-attended show where, from the stage, one could hear everything, even nothing.

"Thinking we catch our breath, head back out."

"God, I hate you." I felt nauseous from the adrenaline and subsequent exhaustion. "You ever think there's a reason no one else is out?"

"Yeah, 'cause Rich runs the shit. The Man wants to surf, that's what's up. That's what happens."

"What are you on… what are you taking?"

"What?"

"What are you on?"

"Adrenaline, bro. That's what I'm on. You talking about?"

"No way you have that much energy. Suboxone, what?"

"No! Fuck, no. Herbs and shit, same as you, fucker. Told you when we got here, this is what I'm meant to do. Built for this shit." He paused and sniffed. "It's what God wants."

"Oh my god." I turned onto my side to look at him, see whether he was serious. He was. "God?"

"Yeah. What, you the only one who gets messages from God? Man, fuck you," he shrugged, picked at the sand and blew some snot and salt water from his nostrils, the stringy remains sticking onto the leg of his wetsuit. "Racist motherfucker."

"What?"

"You heard me. What, a Black man can't want to surf the rest of his life, gotta be on something?"

"Oh, for fuck's sake, Donny. What are you talking about?"

"That's your problem. You don't know what I'm talking about. Keep up. Shit should be obvious."

"You're serious?"

"What I said."

"So, thirty years of grief over The In Between. 'It's what we're meant to do,' and I 'fucked it all up.' Now three whole days in rehab, three: you're only meant to surf, that's what God wants, and I'm a racist."

"I don't make the rules, man. What can I say?"

"Say you're high I guess."

"Oh, calm down ya old Serbian hen. I'm just fucking with ya. Not really. Seriously though. Don't be so sensitive, shit's racist." He looked at me out of the corner of his eye, grinned sardonic, nodded to the outside break.

A set of incoming waves lined up tall out of the blue. Rich and Hana were a few feet apart. They passed on both the first and the second set but dug hard for the third.

"She's gonna snake him. Watch," Donny said.

He was right. Rich had the inside position, perfectly in the pocket, but Hana took off anyways. It was a beautiful wave, blue and green, circular and free flowing, in perfect time; seconds is all it was, but it seemed to unfold forever. Down the face they went together. With a slight stall, Rich hung in the pocket and waited for Hana to make a choice. She did not waste time. With an elegant and aggressive arc, she pulled the bottom turn and pushed up hard for a lip smash against the crest of the wave. As she did, Rich thrust forward beneath her and, with an incredible amount of speed, ripped through her wake, getting out in front of the wave's shoulder for a long and powerful cutback; '70s style soul with form and grace. Hana hit the lip and caught air. Donny yelled out in admiration, "Hana!" As she pulled the drop and came back down, Rich had finished his cutback and was readying for the wave's momentum to again propel him forward. Hana's options were now limited, and she jumped onto Rich's back. Together they bounced until the wave sucked both them and their boards up and over the falls. It was ugly. Both of their leashes snapped; the boards shot high into the air.

Donny and I stood up to gain a better view.

Rich was the first to pop up out of the water, his black wetsuit visible in the whitewash. He looked around, fierce and frantic, for Hana. She popped up next to him and, with the palm of her hands, took numerous swipes at his head. He barely put up his arms to defend himself. After multiple blows, resigned that she would not stop, he slowly swam away from Hana and toward the shore. She followed and grabbed at his legs. Behind them, another large wave approached. They both kicked hard to make the take-off and do what Donny and I had done: bodysurf into and through the trough. Rich went straight down on his belly and, like a submarine, he bounced down the face of the wave. Hana went sideways for the closeout and disappeared into the wave's cratered armpit. We lost sight. Rich's black wetsuit again emerged from the mountainous whitewash. He had somehow managed to maintain position on his belly. To keep his momentum and make it through the trough, he swam with the stroke of a furious butterfly.

"Beast!" Donny said in awe.

Hana arose out of the wash. With a quick flip of her hair, she swam strong, freestyle, and caught a cleanup set. This time she went straight down on her belly, same as Rich had done, to make it all the way in, her tanned body naked against the white foam.

In the trough, both of their boards floated side by side, aimless and silent, pointing true north. Rich ducked out of the now waning whitewash and, with a light breaststroke, swam slowly into the deep of the trough and toward the floating surfboards. Once there, he rested with an arm on each board and caught his breath. We made slight eye contact. He shook his head, embarrassed. Hana swam into the trough. Before she got any closer, Rich lightly pushed her board toward her. It was a kind gesture, a waving of the white flag, if also a move in self-defense. He did not wait for another interaction. He turned and, with one arm still on his board, waded onto the shore.

Donny ran down the sandbar to meet him.

Rich waved him away graciously as if to say, *Not now*. He looked to me, nodded up to the Heights, "Have some things to do. Come and get you later."

Donny bowed his neck confused, affronted. He looked up to me, raised his palms and mouthed the words, "Fuck does that mean?"

It meant he hadn't been invited to dinner at the Turley's. It also meant that, despite his inconsistencies, his newfound God plans did not include me leaving Dover.

He wanted me to stay.

"Going home," I said, weak, guilty almost, the sound of the ocean overbearing.

"What?"

"Leaving."

He pointed to his ears and walked back toward me.

"I said, 'I'm leaving.' I'm going home."

His face fell flat.

Behind him, in the trough, Hana sat up on her board; her hands were lightly lapping in and out of the water, effortless, not an ounce of waste in her movements or on her body, just a lean and supple vessel in its element. Connected. Ferocious.

I couldn't hold her gaze. I was embarrassed by her understanding of the situation, her obvious disdain, her nakedness, not her body but her clarity, and her illness, and her direct connection to source. No filler, no filter; felt like it ripped right through me, exposing not just the hole that existed within, but a seemingly unlimited vast of nothingness born by years, no, decades of degradation.

She smoothly arched her back, slid down on her board, and began a slow paddle toward the outside break.

Donny ran up the sandbar and brushed by me, violent and purposeful, to grab his board. Under his breath, "Sellout motherfucker."

"Donny," I said feeble, knowing he would not be satisfied by my words, only by action, by getting what he wanted. I knew that feeling. Knew it well. How could I blame him?

With his board, he jumped into the trough.

"Donny!" I yelled. "Come on."

He didn't look back.

I sat down on the sandbar, my feet and calves hanging over the crumbling ledge, and watched Donny and Hana both paddle out.

Donny chose to surf The In Between, willfully catching one closeout barrel after the other, and getting pounded each time. Hana pushed north past the outside break and around the jutted rocks of The Bend toward the rugged and unstable shore beneath the cliffs and the long dark shadow of Fairview.

I sat there for hours.
The impressions,
Ruthless.

***

When I got back to the cottage, Rich was there sitting on the cobwebbed Adirondack and reading from his little green book. A golden amber hue from the late afternoon sun encased the cottage. Shadows from the deck's decrepit wooden beams crept through the open front door. My jeans and The In Between t-shirt Donny had given me lay folded on the bed next to the khakis. The bed had been made. Fresh-shaven and barefoot, Rich wore black linen yoga pants and a fitted long sleeve t-shirt, pale blue, cotton, with a thin black Turley 'T' centered from top to bottom splitting his chest plate in two.

"I'm sorry about earlier," he said.

I grimaced but said nothing.

"Nothing really to say, is there?"

"She's your sister."

"Yeah," he cleared his throat and looked out to the ocean. "It's like, every time I think I'm gaining separation from her, mentally, spiritually, even physically, something will happen. Doesn't seem to matter what I do. Therapy, breath work, sweat lodge—try to sweat the spirit out, chase it away—service work, this whole thing, A Return to Dover, even surfing. Just keeps coming. That ever happen to you?"

"No."

"Not even with your mom or… Joy?"

"No."

"No?"

"No."

He paused.

I again wondered if he was consciously or subconsciously pushing me, looking for the weakness, an entry point. Or perhaps he was simply trying to connect and commiserate, and I was doing what I always do: the overthink. *Was I still that distrustful of him, Lord, of people and their generosity?* Yes. Yes, I was. A byproduct perhaps. Too many years under the machine, Los Angeles, watching the gears turn until the big reveal reveals itself yet again; the realization that within every promise of deliverance, the yearning for something more, there is always a catch. I felt for him though. How could I not? He knew what it was like to be gutted, to be both the wrong and the wronged. It was all over him. Powerless. Not only over drugs and alcohol but everything, the people you love, the people you don't even want to love, the feeling and reality, the aches and pains of age, waking up each morning only to realize: This is not going away. This is it.

"Makes sense," he said. "You've been sober so long, doing the work, probably got past that kind of thing a long time ago."

"Takes time," I said, the words awkward, forced, a lie. I wondered if he knew that, too.

"Yeah, or acceptance. I don't think I'm ever gonna get past it, man. For me, it's like clockwork. Even when I was in prison, if something happened to me, I'd get a letter saying something happened to her. It's like… I can't let go and I can't hang on. Stuck, ya know? The In Between. Like it's my dharma. You never feel like that?" he asked again in disbelief.

"I saw her go around The Bend," I said. "Is she at Fairview?"

"No. She should be. Probably. I don't know. She squats up at the house on the hill."

"Crazy Larry's?"

"Yeah."

"Thought that burned down."

"It did. Everything but the concrete, the foundation, those fucking pillars. Remember those? Larry and his monster naked pole dancing thing." He forced a laugh and looked away. "Hate that place. Makes me sick to my stomach. Reminds me of San Francisco, the 'Loin, all the graffiti and trash. Feces. I want to rebuild over there. Dad does, too. We brought in a bunch of developers. They said that with all the erosion up there, the different soils, no one will touch it."

"Maybe it's for the best."

"Yeah, I don't know about that. It's strange though, the soil thing, it's the exact opposite of the Heights. They had a name for it, the kind of coastline we have."

"Discordant."

"Yeah, discordant. How'd you know that, your Dad teach you?"

"I do read."

"Sorry. That was stupid of me. You have a PhD. Fuck. I forget that."

"It's not that, it's just—"

"No, I know, I know. I'm just messing. Your Dad did know everything though."

"Yeah."

"Honestly, I think just being around you, some part of me feels like I did when we were kids, like a euphoric recall or something, like nothing has changed. And sometimes I think that's the way I want it, everything to remain the same… as it was." He dipped deep into the mud of the feeling, his dark eyes welled red, took a deep breath to pull himself out. He stood and set the book down on top of the wooden rail in between us, his voice shaky with emotion. "At some point, most of that area is coming down. The Shack and

Retributions will be covered in dirt, sand, eventually the ocean. Just a matter of when."

"And who will be up there when it happens."

"You want to know what's weird though, really weird? The developers think Fairview will remain up there. They say the ground it's on is just like the ground in the Heights. Hardened. Isn't that crazy? Everything else will look like it does down in Huntington—a long stretch of sand—except one tall cliff with Fairview on top. You imagine that? An insane asylum."

"I can, actually."

"Why, because of what happened to L.A.?"

I nodded, Yes.

"What kind of world, you know?" he continued. "I mean, what kind of Science is that? What does that say when the only thing that stands the test of time is fucking Fairview?"

"And the Heights."

"Yeah, right. The Heights and Fairview."

"It's crazy."

"You don't visit your mom, do you?"

I ripped the Velcro strap from around my neck and unzipped the wetsuit. A small gust of wind came through, the air cool on my now exposed backside. "Nice transition."

"Oh, I didn't mean—"

"I made my peace with her a long time ago."

"You think she feels the same?"

"You pushing me, Rich? That what this is, some kind of test?"

He came back soft, firm. "I'm just asking if you think she feels the same."

"She doesn't have the option of making peace. Making peace is a quality-of-life event."

"I don't disagree with that. It's harsh, but—"

"Yeah, like life. You know that."

There was a pause. My defensiveness, sensitivity, made me sick to my stomach. And it wasn't because he asked me about my mother, it was more the feelings the questions conjured, the helplessness, the lack of control. Somewhere down the line of recovery, I learned there are going to be things we carry; things that won't fully heal; that were I to continue to excavate that pain, that trauma, for too long that it would consume me; its voracity and appetite that insatiable. 'How far down the rabbit hole are you willing to go?' a gentle therapist once asked. Before I could answer, the therapist quickly followed with, 'Not everyone returns.'

"I do know that," Rich said. "And I'm not judging. I only ask because I don't know what I would do if Hana was committed. I think about it all the time though, that maybe it's for the best. Then I think about my mom, how I'd give it all… all this," he raised his palms as if all of Dover were his to give, "to see her. Be with her. Like she was. All of us together. Like we were."

I had half a thought to tell him that he was lucky his mother died. She didn't have to endure his prison sentence, and he didn't have to endure her endurance; didn't have to see the look of love and hope, fear and terror, rage and anger and self-blame in her eyes (the latter probably being the worst, the hardest to let go of) as she visited him over and over and over again in prison. It was the same look that I bore during my visits to my mother at Fairview. I felt for him. How could I not? Sometimes, it's easier to revere the past as something it never was than to accept the randomness of it all. The subsequent acute awareness reveals a grotesque lack of control that can often be too much to bear.

The note from Joy flashed across my mind. Where was it? The khakis pocket. Fuck. My adrenaline surged and my stomach groaned aloud. Did Rich read it? Was he even in the cottage or did he have someone else come in and clean up? I set the nose of the board down on the wooden deck and, with my ring finger, lightly tapped the palm of my hand 3X.

"What does she do up there? How does she eat?" I asked.

"She squats. Has a tent, a burner, all of it. Whatever she wants, really. Dad brings her food and clothes. Medication. She won't take it, probably gives it away or sells it."

"Enabler?"

"Yeah. He knows it, too. But he brings it anyway. He can't stop. And I can't stop him. I tried. Doesn't work."

"Yeah, they end up hating you for telling them what they already know is true. I'm sorry, man," I said, looking at the khakis in the cottage.

One, two, three.

One, two, three.

One, two, three.

"Yeah… we share that, don't we," he said. But it wasn't a question; it was a resignation. He breathed in deep and exhaled loudly; again, clearing his throat.

"I should shower," I said.

"Yeah. Yeah, we should get going. Gotta get up in the barrel before the tide gets too high, and Helen gets her drink on."

"She a drunk?"

"No, I don't think so. She's never missed a day of work in her life. It does bring out a sort of weirdness though. You'll see."

"Someone going to get Donny or?"

"No. Why?"

"He's still in rehab, right?"

"It's not a prison. If he wants out, it's his choice. He needs choice. Gives him a chance to own his recovery. Build self-esteem."

"I don't think he wants out." (I didn't really believe that. I didn't know what to believe with Donny. Never do with a newcomer. I said it anyways, as if on reflex.) "But seems like a little more time would be appropriate before he gets to make decisions for himself."

"I wouldn't discount him. He made a decision to get here."

"Not really."

"If he didn't want to be here, he wouldn't be here, Jimmy. You know that. Besides, the whole jail rehab thing, that's not what we're about here. We see Donny as… different; his Science is different. Have to flex with it. If I put rules around him, he'll bounce for sure. I mean, he may bounce anyways, but it won't be because of rules. Do that, it takes away his dignity. His right to choose. Can't take that away. It's the only thing he has left."

"He's catching closeout barrels in The In Between. What kind of dignity is that?"

He shrugged.

"You don't see that as self-destructive?"

"Of course it is. But it's better to get the anger out at Retributions than on someone else, or on himself. It's like a tell it to the mountain thing. Mountain's not gonna listen. He'll figure it out. Trust. It'll probably help him sleep tonight."

"Probably going to drown."

"That guy is not gonna drown. He's too good of a surfer, always has been."

And there it was, Lord, again with my inconsistencies, my hypocrisy. Maybe Rich was right. I wanted Donny to get clean in the way that I got clean. But that's not how it works. I was blinded, a hostage of my own experience, and my humanity was being thrown back into my face. Real time. What I give is what I get. What I see is what I am. A human being. Ugh.

An ugly Truth unending.

"We can talk more about Donny later. Got a long drive south to L.A. tomorrow. Does he know you're leaving?"

I nodded, Yes.

"How'd that go?"

One, two, three.

One, two, three.

One, two, three.

"It's gonna be alright, Jimmy. You'll see." He nodded to the cottage door. "I got the jeans and The In Between shirt cleaned. Can't believe you still have that shirt, let alone fit into it."

"It's Donny's."

"He really cares, you know? About you, The In Between, the music we made. Well, really the music you two made."

"It was all of us, Rich. Never the same without you."

He looked down and away.

"I doubt that's true. But thank you for saying it."

"There's more to a band than music."

"Go on and get showered."

As I walked through the door and got a closer look at the khakis, I could see an ever so small edge of the note sticking out the front pocket.

"There really was a time, wasn't there?" Rich said aloud.

"Yeah. There really was."
Et id tempus abiit.

Prologue (2)

I MET HELEN WU in the fifth grade. She sat upfront in class, had short black hair with bangs, braces with neckgear, and won every scholastic and sports competition offered at Dover Elementary. She steered far from the smoking-cigarettes-after-school-Wooden- Park crowd; far from punk rock, or new wave, or heavy metal, or anything resembling what was once referred to as a defiant or delinquent identity. And she steered very, very far from the comedic laissez-faire surf and skate crowd to which her brother (who was so talented at skateboarding he arguably defined, and defied the logic of, the now ubiquitous term, Air) belonged.

When the braces came off and the bangs grew out into a long luxurious sheen, Helen emerged as what one might describe as an early-80s prototype Sports Illustrated model. Not that she would have any of that noise; its simultaneous exultation degradation trap; its limited identity based on nothing (to her at least) but genes which were simply passed on down the line. No. It was beneath both her intellect and her self-esteem. Can't say I blame her. Not then, and certainly not now.

The last time I recall seeing her was just before she went away to college on a full ride scholarship to Stanford.

She was standing alone in the Wooden Park shooting arrows into a target she had hung on an old oak tree. Awkward, as always, I waved to her. I don't know why I did that. Who waves at people? It's stupid. Just keep walking. But, with her bow drawn tight as the ponytail sticking out the back of her head, she acknowledged my fumbling gesture with an ever so slight upward nod so as to not lose focus on her target. The sound of the arrow piercing the paper bullseye and entering the womb of the old oak tree startled me, so much so that I shook as if from a cold chill.

Chapter Two: Two Roads Diverged

THERE IS NOTHING like a warm shower after surf. Nothing. Were it not for Rich waiting out front, the incoming tide and the barrel ride up the cliff to the Heights, I would have stayed in that shower forever.

It makes me happy that you are here. I hope you stay…

—Joy

Makes me happy. Fuck does that mean? I counted to three 3X and got dressed. Clean jeans, clean t-shirt. Felt good to be out of the khakis. More like myself. The surf should have brought on hunger, but my stomach was still unsettled; my breath was full and heavy as if there weren't enough air. And in a way there wasn't. The humidity in Dover Shores, being that near the water, was much different than the arid and parched particulate smog heat of Los Angeles and The Vortex.

I again read the partially torn note, "I hope you stay…", then carefully folded it along its edges so as to not disturb its form and put it in the front pocket of my jeans.

The return of the counting gave me cause for concern: going to dinner; seeing Senior after all these years, let alone Joy if she was going to be there; the embarrassment if I began to count aloud, or with my fingers; not to mention the scars. That said, I felt pretty good from the endorphin rush of surfing and with Donny in rehab… mission accomplished. One step closer to home. And I was looking forward to seeing Senior. He was good to me during some very tough years. I wondered whether he resented me for not doing the same in return and standing by Rich, or even him, during the murder trial. I wouldn't blame him if he did. He had reached out numerous times. But I was newly sober and fearful of his angry, mostly drunken, voice messages. Not fearful of him, mind you, but fearful of myself and my unresolved inclinations toward co-dependency and justified anger to the injustices of the world, perceived or real, of which he was clearly struggling with.

Also, I wasn't entirely sure Rich going to prison was, in fact, an injustice. The pure rage he had in his eyes that night in San Francisco; it was fire, indignant and animalistic, as if a switch had been turned on and he was no longer in his body, but rather he was his body. I didn't know if it was the beating he took from the cops, the steroids he and the skinheads he was hanging around with were taking, or a consensual sadomasochistic ritual gone too far leaving Brandy dead.

But something wasn't right.

And Joy, despite the conflicted feelings the note conjured, I wasn't so emotionally disabled that I couldn't recognize the Truth. Yes, she was my wife. My family. The voice that lingered. But more than that, she was now just another newcomer bouncing from one fix to another. It didn't matter whether she and Rich were real, or if they were able to do what ninety-nine percent of all newcomers cannot do: stay together. It would still be better than her being on the street; and for now, it meant an end to my relentless wonder and worry of when I would get the call, her having been found dead, or raped, or beaten, or all the above, in a tent somewhere in Hollywood or downtown. And no politician was going to make that phone call. No hustler for votes, no telemarketer, or canvasser, or social media savior, claiming that dignity for the unhoused is to live unencumbered in a patchwork of duct-tape tents lining the sun-scorched streets of good old hospitable and loving L.A. is going make that phone call. No. It's going to be some underpaid PTSD cop, possibly the same cop the vote hustler was trying to defund and—how's this for irony—put out on the street.

Rich and Joy together?

So be it.

I know what you're thinking, a little chilly. But that's the thing about being clean and sober long term: one learns to find the positive in disappointment. A marathon is what it is, a lived Burkean parlor, a free flowing eurythmic, a dance of spirit and constraint.

That's Science.

That's Truth.

The problem is that Truth waxes and wanes and often becomes so diluted through all the one-day-at-a-times that it sometimes seems impossible to differentiate fact from fiction.

In other words, as the man (Descartes) once said:

"*And yet I realize how prone my mind is to error.*"

Rest.

***

Rich and I walked mostly silent down to the shoreline then south through the tidepools, a long labyrinth of rough granite and smooth sandstone. It was high tide and the water was cold. The whitewash rushed in fast and hard over my bare feet. Rich yelled something and, even though we were close in proximity to one another, I could not hear what he said over the roar of the ocean.

I jumped onto a tall rock and rolled my jeans up to the knee and waited for the tide to ebb. Beneath me were a rainbow of sea anemones and starfish, mussels and barnacles; purple and green crabs crawling side-to-side in search of protection.

As the tide sucked out, and the sound of the waves slightly dulled, Rich said loudly, “See who can make it to the barrel first?”

It was a game we used to play as kids. I laughed.

“Come on, man. Be fun.”

“Nah. Don’t want to make you feel bad,” I said.

“You were pretty quick back in the day, but… I saw you surfing today, bro,” he chided. “Not too worried.”

I nodded and then quickly jerked my body as if to start the race. Rich flinched just enough to be off balance. And that’s when I took off! One rock at a time, no time for second guessing, I leapt fluid and smooth and, as I did, laughed like a child.

“You ain’t gonna make it, old man!” he said from behind.

One, two, three.

One, two, three.

One, two, three.

I leapt, and I leapt, and I leapt.

“You ain’t gonna make it!” he said again, now laughing with his own excitement.

One, two, three.

One, two, three.

One, two, three.

I leapt, and I leapt, and I leapt.

He drew close and taunted, “You. Ain’t. Gonna. Make it!”

My lungs felt heavy with elation and exertion, adrenaline and age; my mouth filled with saliva. I tried to keep pace but felt myself slowing.

One, two, three.

One, two, three.

One, two, three.

I leapt, and I leapt, and I leapt, then slipped on a rock and fell into a pit of turbulent whitewash. I pushed myself up onto another rock. But it was too late to catch Rich.

One slip is all it takes isn’t it, Lord?

Yes.

I slowly did the walk-of-shame and made my way over to Rich who stood on a large obelisk of a rock at the base of the cliff, a towering three-hundred fifty-foot vertical saltine wall.

“What took you so long?” he said, a knowing grin.

“Yeah, yeah, yeah.”

“Need to get your lungs back, bro. We ain’t done yet. Still gotta get in the barrel.”

Built into the cliff was the barrel, a bronze funicular open-air car on two shining steel rails that rose all the way up to the Heights.

“How do we even get up there?”

“See that alcove? That’s the entry point. Get up there, jump onto the ladder and into the barrel. One, two, three. Easy.”

The ladder was old and beat up, rusted and bent; its ends jagged and pocked with holes. The middle rung was snapped in two, as if someone had taken a rock or hammer so as to not allow others passage.

“Doesn’t look like much of a ladder,” I said.

"Keeps the kooks away."

"Man, I can't get up on that thing."

"Sure you can. Looks worse from down there. Just watch how I hit that top rung and then use the cliff to push off. That's the only hard part, ladder to barrel."

"Yeah, only hard part," I said sarcastic.

"You scared?"

"Just go."

In one constant fluid motion, he leapt up onto the alcove then onto the top rung of the rusted ladder, which made an awful sound of bending steel, and into the barrel. He looked down at me with the look of a man affirmed. "See? Easy."

He did make it look easy, and I did feel pressure. Kind of silly, all these years later to still care about, and fall victim to, other people's opinions. And yet, still.

"Better get going before that tide comes in," he said.

I turned. Another rush of whitewash was coming toward me. I wouldn't be able to jump that fast. I lowered my stance so as to not get bowled over. The surge of the water was strong, but I held my ground. The force of the whitewash pounded and splashed against the rocks. My jeans were soon wet up to my waist.

"You need some help?"

Embarrassed—any rookie knows to watch their back for rogue waves in the tidepools—I felt a flash of resolve and followed Rich's lead; rock to rock to ledge, up the ladder and into the barrel. The clunkiness of age was still upon me, but I made it.

"My man," he grabbed my arm and helped steady my gait.

"Not bad for an old man."

"Not bad at all."

The barrel itself was dark brown, a tarnished bronze with enough room for only two people. A Turley 'T' had been cast into the middle of the floor.

"Haven't used this thing in a while," he said.

"How long is a while?"

"Don't worry. Everything's up to code. Those old-timers may have been salty, but they knew what they were doing." He pushed a green button multiple times, a melodic Morse code. There was a sudden jolt. The car floor vibrated and shook violently, then slowly leveled out and began its ascent up to the Turley's home in the Heights. "We replaced the steel rails," he said loudly over the moan of the car. "But we couldn't replace any of the harnesses, or anything already built into the cliff. Nothing. Not even the ladder."

"Risk the whole thing coming down?"

"Yeah. The cliff, all of it." He laughed. "But don't worry. I'm sure we'll make it."

With no wind and no fog, we rose up and up and up. The early October sun reached the horizon. We had an unobstructed view of the Pacific in all its promise, all its imaginings; its colors and contours, a deep blue entity teeming with who knows what underneath. To the north and south, far as the eye could see along the coastline, were sparkling and majestic cliffs saturated in shades of red and orange and yellow; its darkened crevices filled with undulating and foreboding shadow. It was everything that everyone always thinks of when they think of California. Even Fairview, in the distance across The Shores, with its looming black monolithic structure, was tempered in cinnamon, a warm vermillion, like something out of a dream.

"Sure is beautiful," Rich said. "And the best part, it's ours."

It took a second for my eyes to adjust to the height and the bold glare of the setting sun. The "ours" comment was not lost on me but, in a way, it did feel like ours. Always did. Not in the literal sense, but in a physical, perhaps even spiritual, sense. Like a song, California, California, that floats ethereal in and through the body leaving a trace of feeling, of longing, of wondering whether its scents, colors, and sounds had become my Science, my DNA. We've eaten its dirt, swallowed its water, procreated in its soil, been pummeled by its fury. What was it if not a habitat and, we, its inhabitants.

Why wouldn't it be in our blood?

We reached the top of the cliff. The car stopped abruptly, again with a sudden jerk. Still transfixed on the sunset and my thoughts, I lost balance and with both hands quickly grabbed the rails. I stared straight down the vertical cliff into the rocks and the violence of the crashing waves below. My knees slightly buckled. The car reversed onto a platform for exit.

"Look at Retributions; just keeps getting better," Rich said.

He was right. Endless lines of perfection. Waves upon waves upon waves. Rising darkness contrasted with trailing lines of whitewash surging maniacal toward its end in The In Between.

We exited the car and walked out onto a thin gravel path filled with dark grey stones. They were soft and forgiving on my bare feet, warm from a full day's sun. Along each side of the path were tall and manicured Italian cypress trees, lush and green; the dirt below was dark and smelled rich with minerals. Above our heads hung translucent strings of light, the filament soft and yellow, seductive. One thousand three hundred sixty-nine strings of light am I right, Mr. Ellison?

And yet still…

The trail forked into a circle filled with tiny beige pebbles. We stopped. With my jeans wet, I caught a chill. In the middle of the circle there was a large fountain with a variation of the Turley 'T' sculpture. Water flowed smooth and easy up through the cross, out from top of the 'T' and back down into a shimmering low-lit dark pool.

"Two roads diverged?" Rich said, forcing a laugh. His face flushed red as if he was anxious. The whitened scar of his now removed swastika tattoo shone from underneath the red of his neck. "You nervous?"

"No." I lied. "You?"

"A little, yeah." He looked me in the eye. "Your call. We can turn around."

I thought of the note, then of Senior, what it might say about me if I were to bounce yet again. Part of me thought that, outside of the note from Joy, perhaps I was only here to make an amends to Rich and to Senior for not sticking around, not being loyal to those who had been loyal to me; that perhaps Donny was merely a conduit to get me here; that I could finally rid myself of the lingering guilt I worked so hard to deny all these sober years later.

Could it be that simple? And what would that even look like? An apology? I already apologized to Rich. What did I owe to Senior? Or is it just me, yet again, being unable to accept my humanity, that I wasn't perfect in all my affairs, that I had to for once take care of myself first. I wondered whether an amends would be just another opportunistic grab at relieving guilt (my own) at the expense of others. *No easy answers are there, Lord*? No. Only one way to find out.

I counted to three 3X.

"No. I want to see your dad."

"Okay. Left, or right?"

"Huh?"

He nodded to the fountain and the circle. "Left, or right?"

"Left."

We continued walking along the pebbled path. They were less forgiving on my feet than the smooth stones. The air was still, filled with moisture and salt. It wouldn't be long before the fog rolled in. Beyond the fountain there was an expansive, well-appointed limestone patio that led directly into the Turley home. Sprawling and two-story, the home was breathtaking, a work of art reminiscent of a Mickey Muennig design. It was at once organic and modern, a twist on the vintage California Ranch style home. Slightly concave in the middle with tall paned glass windows from floor to ceiling, a haunting golden light emanated from within, a perfect balance of both comfort and wealth. It was stunning. Mesmerizing. So much so, I nearly walked myself into a small dark wading pool.

"You sure you're ready for this?"

I nodded, Come on, man. Let's go.

From the center out, Rich opened the tall and thick sliding glass doors. Waves of air pressure filled my ears and were soon followed by the sound of "The whole world may be on fire; I don't fucking care! That's not what I pay you for. The short provides the push. That's the coil, the tension for the stock price to move. Please, do your job. Don't make me ask again."

We entered the living room.

Hand on hip, Helen tossed her cell phone onto the couch, a plush white sectional, with two chaise lounges, that horseshoed around a three-inch thick blue-glass coffee table. On top of the table were an array of vases filled with purple, pink, and blue orchids. "Jimmy Marsanovic," she said cooly. "How have you been?"

"Good. Fine," I said, awkward like a child. "How have you been?"

Good? Fine? How have you been? Please kill me.

"Busy," she said matter of fact, a raise of her hands to the surroundings followed by a small pause and a deep stare into the scars that lined my face. "I'd ask you to sit, but you're all wet. There are some khakis in the guest bedroom. Rich, will you show him?"

Rich closed the sliding glass doors. "He doesn't like the khakis."

"What's wrong with khakis? You'd rather be wet all night?"

"No, it's fine. I can change."

"See, Rich," she said. "He can change."

He nodded somewhat reluctantly and then said to me, "I'll put the jeans in the dryer. Be done before dinner."

"Shake them out first," Helen said. "Or better, wash them."

"They just were washed," Rich said.

She shrugged. Her shoulders were strong and broad. She wore a black satin Nehru jacket with embroidered, pearl-white tufted paisley high to the neck. "I don't want sand in the dryer. I hate sand," she said.

"We live at the beach, and Helen hates sand."

"We live above the beach. There's a difference. Thank you."

"Where's Dad?"

"He'll be out in a minute. Joy's helping him." She turned to me. "Did Rich tell you that he's in a wheelchair now?"

"He doesn't need to be in that thing."

"It's because of his surfing," she said to me.

"It's not because of surfing," Rich said. "This whole place is because of his surfing. It's because of his ego."

Helen raised an eyebrow but said nothing.

"Come on, Jimmy." Rich led me into an amber hued hallway with cream white carpet that felt like warm velvet on my cold feet. The walls were adorned—no, curated—with family pictures, framed and 35mm, a few proof sheets thrown in for good measure, capturing an era, a culture of California that no longer exists: boogie boards and blue sky, Coppertone tan lines, metal bicycles with scruffy-hair neighborhood kids, girls and boys in long socks and short shorts riding crude skateboard ramps built with stolen wood from some construction site (got arrested for that, 30 days with a hoe on the side of the road, 14 years old, wasn't the first time, wasn't the last), nails sticking out the sides, ready for young knees to be ripped to the bone, the cartilage for all to see; young fathers with beards and bandanas, hand rolled cigarettes, joints I suppose; grandmothers who looked like grandmothers, faces bearing the lines of war, canned food and fallout shelter drills, thwarted desire, avoidant and aware, weary and suspicious of the camera (who wouldn't be?), sitting in aluminum chairs with multi-colored webbing made of God knows what; mothers, wives and cousins, girlfriends in cut-off jean shorts, red, white or blue doo-rags, drinking Coors beer from a can at a barbecue with a grassy knoll; potato sack races, flailing limbs, tumbling humans smiling, laughing unkempt, unaware and uncaring of their toothy teeth, unknowing of the early incarnation of what would become a surf empire; from garages filled with cans of resin and blanks of foam and fiberglass cloth, to a grommet-laden 80's Main Street mall, to ringing the bell on Wall Street. It was a museum, a poem, a story, a cascading victory felled and filled with the stuff of life.

"Hana take these?" I asked.

"Most of 'em."

I felt transported. "It's incredible. The color. Quality. Perspective. It's all there. All of it."

"I'm so glad we had that time. Ya know? Kids don't get that anymore, that kind of freedom."

"No. No, they don't."

"Pictures now… everyone's looking into their phones. Have to escape somewhere, I guess."

"It's true. No release point with tech though. No space for the body. It's like a pressure cooker. All mental."

"Yeah, it's a loop. For sure. Reminds me of prison. Check these out."

At the far end of the wall next to a bedroom door there was an 8x10, black and white, of the first In Between gig. *Jesus, Lord.* Could I have ever been that young? Next to the picture, in its own frame was a solo shot of Donny behind his kit, alive and well, fierce and in the zone. It held me, as all good drummers are wont to do, control and manipulate the flow of time. Dictate terms.

Attack life. Not the other way around.

"This will sound cliché, but as bad as things got for me, I wouldn't change a thing."

His comment surprised me. "Not even prison?"

"No," he said flatly. "I mean, trust me, I get it; it's easy to say that now. But it made me who I am. It's my Science. Can't change it. Wouldn't want to, either."

"Science as destiny, that what The Science is?"

He sensed my discomfort. "I don't believe we all came from some planet, or I'm on some divine mission, if that's what you mean."

"That's not what I mean," I said.

"Well, what do you mean?"

"You said, 'your path' and I got the feeling you felt like this was all part of a master plan. Like it's preordained."

"You don't think there's anything, do you?"

"Lot of evidence to the contrary."

He paused. "We see what we want to see. Doesn't mean it's Truth though."

"So, you were supposed to go to prison?"

"That's what everyone asks. It's a little more mutable than that, little more Zen. I think there are simultaneous Truths. Getting a raw deal doesn't preclude divinity; two sides of the same coin. It's what makes the whole thing special. Ya know? The possibilities out of the contradictions. A rose out of the mud. Gotta embrace it, man. Hold onto it. It's all we got."

"You didn't answer the question though."

He grinned and shook his head in both wonder and amusement. "Fucking Jimmy, always pushing to the bottom of things. The way I see it is this: I either accept the totality of my life, or I suffer. That's Science. That's Truth. Prison is a part of my Science. So, what am I going to do about it? If I live in the past, I die in the present. I can't live in an existential question, or some kind of 'what if' scenario. That's privilege. Doomscroll privilege. You know? Not to mention, sloth. It's like, you know when people say we're all connected?"

"Yeah."

"Mostly, I think that's Truth. But plants and animals don't live in the past. They don't live in a question. We're the ones that assign significance and spin it into a tale. Some dumb Hollywood story. Have I always enjoyed the path? Am I going to say I'm happy it happened? No. Fuck no. Nearly killed me. But so what, everyone's path nearly kills them. The struggle of whether we go left or right, I think, is an illusion; it can delay things but… this life or the next, we get to where we're going."

"Where's that?"

"Helping people. You know that. It's what it's all about. A return to source." He shrugged. "A Return to Dover. Return to each other. That's Science."

And I did know that didn't I, Lord? And I was uncomfortable, wasn't I?

Yes.

Rich had the faith of the dying, the kind only a newcomer could muster. A part of me envied him. And in the end, he could have called it anything he wanted: Science, Zen, Allah, Buddha, Krishna, Christ, Ra, God. But I did know that. And yet I could barely recall the last time I had helped someone, so lost was I in self, in ideals and self-pity, symbols and scars and, yes, the past. Sure, there was Donny. I helped him get to Dover. But that doesn't count. That was then. Yesterday. The past. And I'd gone too far and too few in between without my medicine, without helping someone. Donny was right, those college kids don't care about English, or literature, they just think that shit is racist. And I certainly wasn't helping people in the way that Rich was; he was helping rooms filled with people. He spent twenty-two years in prison and found a way out of what I was clearly stuck inside of: self. Did it matter whether he was right or if it was Truth? He had more hope with less reason. And what was I doing other than whining? He must have seen it, my regression; it made me uncomfortable. Exposed. I returned my gaze to the solo picture of Donny; then, in my mind's eye, to him alone catching closeout barrels in The In Between. Blood rushed to my forehead. Tinnitus rang in my left ear. I felt heavy, like I had sunken deep into something I could not pull myself out of.

"You alright? Looking pretty intense."

"Lot of history here."

"Sure is, and we survived. Lot of people didn't. Should be proud of it."

He was right, but somehow, I wasn't.

"You sure you're alright?"

"Yeah, I'm fine. Just hungry."

"Me too. Come on." He walked me into the room. "Hana stays here sometimes. The clothes are in the dresser, top drawer. I'll be out in the living room."

"The living room?"

"Yeah… where Helen was."

"That's a living room?"

"Not really," he laughed. "I don't know what it is, but that's where we'll be. Oh, and the dryer is in the hallway, behind the shutter doors."

"What about the sand?"

"Don't worry about Helen. Just put 'em in."

He closed the door. His animosity with Helen was clear but I said nothing. What was there to say? Nothing worse than people prying into other people's business, as if they knew what was best. I closed my eyes and took a deep breath, counted to three 3X.

Hana's room appeared strangely bland, a stark contrast to the rest of the home. The walls were a muted mustard with an off-white trim. The bed was centered against the wall and had a worn-out mauve-grey paisley comforter that was not nearly long enough to cover the discolored box spring or the uneven, slanted black metal frame on plastic wheels. There were a variety of throw pillows propped against the wall, all of them fringed and also paisley, some variation of brown.

Above the bed, within arm's reach, in a cheeky gold frame was what appeared to be an original Nagel, Duran Duran's *Rio* album cover. It had been signed. I wondered if the signature was real; I had heard there were so many fakes. Knowing Hana, it was probably authentic. She loved Duran Duran. And who wouldn't? she would ask. Who in their right mind wouldn't love Duran Duran? I stood there for a moment and observed the lines, the detachment, the promise of a woman unmoored from societal perception and expectation; it seemed oddly fresh and vibrant, current even. And when I thought about it, Hana was right. Who wouldn't love Duran Duran? Who wouldn't throw it all away, all the serious homeless, druggie, art-is-dead, political, tech, gender, race, identity, climate disaster concerns for a *cherry ice cream smile* and the dream of an illustrated woman unencumbered by man?

I counted to three 3X and went to the oak dresser to find the khakis. The dresser had been completely sanded down. It must have taken a long time, a lot of grinding and scraping, patience and persistence, to get it in that kind of shape. It was ready for the finish. Wedged beneath the vanity mirror, clouded by dust and sanded oak particles, fanning out wide like a hand of cards, were several Polaroids of Rich and Hana when they were young: children climbing and loving and happily goofing around with their mother. Love in their hearts. It moved me. I peeled my eyes and shook my head, took a long deep breath to keep it together. *Rio* was the album, Duran Duran was the band, the year Mrs. Turley died. She never got to see The In Between or see the explosion of the surf industry. She also never had to see Rich go to prison, or Hana go to Fairview. Probably better that way. For everyone. If the cancer hadn't killed her, Rich in prison and Hana in Fairview would have.

I wondered what Rich thought about that, The Science of his mother. Does it all still work out, a move toward helping one another? A Return to Dover? Did it even matter what I thought? Why so judgmental all the time?

Life kills. Them's the rules.

I opened one of the dresser drawers. Inside there were multiple sets of beige khaki pants and beige long sleeve khaki shirts. I took off my wet jeans and, as I did, caught a glimpse of myself naked in the mirror. A scarred and gangled creature stared back at me. I thought of my little hovel in The Vortex, the Serbian graveyard where my ancestors lay in wait—won't be long now—the chickens laying their eggs; the city, the citadel, the recycled plastic acropolis formerly known as Los Angeles, gutted by fire and drought, inequality, over-educated privileged rage, unmoored from compromise, from anything other than the desire to promote self, establish identity, the one identity that outshines all the other identities, everyone clamoring for respect and stature, to forever stamp their victimhood, their humanity upon the stark and homeless L.A. dust.

I pulled off The In Between t-shirt and took another long look at myself in the mirror. *Jesus, Lord*. What am I doing? Not much time left. I put on the khakis. Strangely, they felt good. Clean and warm.

I would want my record collection.

Were I to stay.

Rest.

***

I re-entered the living room.

The living room.

The living room.

Joy stood behind Senior. They were in conversation with Helen who stood off to the side making a drink in front of a floor-to-ceiling mirrored bar. Senior was sitting in a wheelchair. He wore black satin pants and a black Nehru jacket very similar to Helen's, only there was no white embroidery around the neck—it was all black. Behind them a thick and fast-moving fog pushed up against the tall paned glass windows and flowed in two distinct directions around the home.

"Heeere's Jimmy," Helen said, making eye contact through the mirror.

"Jimmy!" Senior waved me over.

As I walked toward them, I quickly glanced at Joy. She seemed poised and confident, comfortable and happy; again, wearing her single-breasted ghost white Turley Tencel suit; again, no camisole, no blouse, no bra, nothing but tattoos and enhanced breasts. It shouldn't have bothered me. Who am I to judge? But it did. Her hand rested on Senior's shoulder. Her fingers were aged and gnarled at the knuckle. The engagement ring from Rich sparkled in the room's soft amber light; it was a far stolid cry from the solidarity of the plain black bands we once wore.

"But to finish my thoughts," Senior said, matter of fact. "Vultures. That's what they are. All of 'em. Vultures. Jimmy, come here. Come closer. My eyes are bad. Let me get a look at you."

He held out his hand for a gentlemen's shake. His fingers were long. Our hands slightly missed one another. His hardened nails dug into my wrist as he pulled me in close, a scent of baby shampoo in his long hair and soft beard. He whispered in my ear, "A prodigal son always returns. You are wanted and needed here. Please stay." He let go and gently patted the scars on my face. "Kid hasn't changed at all," he said aloud. "Looks like a million bucks!"

"Someone has a fan," Helen said.

"Yeah, I don't know about that. It's good to see you, too," I said, feeling the weight of a thousand stares, an animal in khakis on display. I had no concrete reason to feel that way, I just did. Perhaps I always just… did.

Senior and I locked eyes. We took in each other's essence with wonderment and recognition, as if no time had passed, no water had run under the bridge. His face had been softened by age and held a faded, almost colorless complexion, a mixture of brown, grey, and white that mirrored the color of his hair. The widow's peak severe, he wore the look of a contented man both tired and frail. Yet underneath the infirmities of age his eyes remained sharp and blue, much like Hana's. But rather than her vacuous and unpredictable crystal-blue hole, Senior's gaze was more that of an old bird of prey—*an old bird of prey, Lord*—one that sees everything.

"That's what music does," he said. "Keeps you young!"

"Jimmy doesn't play music, Dad," Joy said flatly. "He's a teacher now."

My stomach groaned aloud.

"An adjunct professor," Helen said. "I was telling you about it the other day. Like a contractor, but for college."

Senior's eyes widened as if he was confused or trying to focus, to connect me, or his perception of me, with higher education. "What college?" he asked.

"Community… mostly," I said.

"You like that?"

"It's a lot of hustle," I said looking to Joy, an emotional temperature check. She offered no eye contact. Her eyes bore a hole of discontent through my solar plexus. "But… yeah, I like it. It's good for me, keeps me out of trouble."

"Trouble. Now we're talking!"

"Where's Rich?"

"A little business."

"He'll be back soon," Joy said.

It grew quiet. It wasn't the first time that someone, upon hearing that I was a teacher, a professor, adjunct, whatever, had given me that look. I had been getting that look for years. It's the kind of look that asks the recipient, Is everything okay? Did something happen? In other words, what is wrong with you?

In the early years of my transition, I enjoyed seeing the confusion in people's eyes. The contradictions felt more like validation, like punk rock—the ethos, not the product—and right or wrong it made me happy when my mere presence disturbed the perception of others. But not anymore. Not since the stabbing. I guess it really is like my father said, Postojalo je vreme, i to vreme je prošlo. *There was a time, and that time is gone*.

And I had grown.

I had learned that it's not my job to make others feel comfortable by engaging in small talk, so I let the silence remain and returned Joy's icy volley with a long steely stare of my own. Jimmy doesn't play music! Calling him Dad already? Please stay? What does that even mean? Please stay. And why would Senior say that, please stay? A part of me began to wonder if it was Joy who wrote the note. I quickly felt for it in my pocket, but it wasn't there. In my moment of naked and decrepit clarity, standing in front of the mirror in Hana's room, I left the note in the jeans. Again. *What is wrong with me, Lord*? It is such a simple thing.

"Oh!" I blurted out. "I just realized I left the wet jeans on top of the bed. I should go get them."

Helen tilted her head backward in dismay.

"Eh, let 'em dry on their own," Senior said nonplussed.

"No, they're pretty wet. I should—"

"I got 'em," Rich said entering the room, a grin on his face. "Put 'em in the dryer. Helen, you can relax now."

Again, my stomach groaned aloud.

"Everything okay?" Joy asked.

"My stomach, just been off schedule," I said, self-conscious.

Joy shook her head and rolled her eyes. "I was talking to Rich. Everything okay, babe?"

"All good. Business as usual." Rich said.

"You sure?" Senior asked.

"Yep. Couple fires. No big deal."

"Darling," Senior said to Joy. "Will you wheel me over to the couch? I want to watch the fog before dinner."

"You can walk there yourself, Dad," Rich said.

"It's fine, babe. I'm happy to." Joy wheeled Senior over to the couch, another waft of her heavy musk as she passed me by.

"Jimmy, what would you like to drink?" Helen asked, still staring at me through the mirror.

"Get him something with bubbles," Senior said. "Something for his stomach."

"Jimmy, come on," Senior said. "Come sit next to me on the couch."

I followed them to the couch. Senior stood up on his own with no problem from the wheelchair. "Can someone move these flowers from the table? They're blocking my view."

"Jesus, Dad. Anything else?" Rich asked.

"He's not supposed to lift anything over ten pounds," Helen said to Rich.

"Yeah, well that was only supposed to be for the first month. Come on, Dad. You can move those things."

"No, I don't want to risk it," Senior said. "Have to lean and lift."

"Since when have you been afraid of risk? Your whole life is risk."

"I don't make the rules. Is what it is, am I right, Jimmy?" Senior said.

"Yeah, is what it is," I said, playing along, not really knowing what to say.

"*It is what it is* is weak, you ask me," Rich said.

"Everyone heals differently, Son."

"Here, let me help with the flowers," I said.

"No, Jimmy. You come sit with me. Let Rich handle it." Senior sat down in the middle of the couch. Rich and Joy picked up the vases and set them on a table near the hallway. I sat next to Senior. The seat cushions were deep with no real support for my back, so I sat upright at the edge of the couch. With my left hand, so as not to be seen, I began tapping incessant—pinky, ring, middle against my leg:

One, two, three. One, two, three. One, two, three.

One, two, three. One, two, three. One, two, three.

One, two, three. One, two, three. One, two, three.

"I hate this couch," Senior said to me, casual. "Looks nice but that's about it."

Helen walked to the couch and handed Senior a drink. "A Bourbon and Blood for the gentleman." She placed a bar napkin underneath the glass though there were vintage corked coasters on the coffee table. Senior cradled the heavy glass with two hands and slurped at the bloody orange top.

"Enough bitters?" Helen asked.

"Oh yeah," he said, shaking off the sour sting. "No one makes 'em like you, babe. Can you get me some of those pillows for my back?"

"Sure. Jimmy, your Perrier."

My hand trembled as I reached for the small green bottle, also with a napkin underneath. I was alarmed by the shaking, but the napkin helped me to get a better grip. "Thank you."

"Am I the only one drinking?" Senior said aloud.

"Everyone's sober, Dad," Rich said aloud from the hallway.

"Ahh, yes. There is that, isn't there?" He winked at me.

"I may have some wine at dinner," Helen said. "Excuse me, Jimmy." She leaned over me and grabbed three throw pillows, a scent of pungent perfume as she propped the pillows against Senior's back. "That better, babe?"

"Yes, thank you. Rich, Joy. Come sit. The fog is rolling in."

Helen, still standing, took time to adjust her waistline. Her face was youthful, full, barely any lines, yet she wore heavy makeup high to the forehead and low to the neck and the white embroidery of the Nehru jacket. "Jimmy, can you move over a little bit?" I set the bottle of Perrier down and moved to the left. "A little more please. I like to give the old oak tree—"

"Old oak tree?" Senior interrupted.

"Old oak tree, a shoulder rub while we watch the fog."

Senior scoffed playful.

I moved over again, further to the left. Helen kicked off her shiny black high heels, which had been hiding under the length of her satin pants, then curled up behind Senior. The girth of her midriff pushed against the buttons of the Nehru jacket revealing a beige, laced compression bodysuit. The slack in her pants fell flat upon her lanky legs and what had once been long black hair was now short with high bangs, uniform in length, and held together tight by product, accentuating a thinning hairline.

Rich and Joy reentered the living room and lay down on the chaise at the other end of the couch. They put their arms around each other. It grew quiet, all of us looking out into the fog and its smooth dance with, and against, the tall paned glass.

"Tell us about the fog, hon," Helen said. "What do you see tonight?"

Rich looked to me with a wink in his eye that said welcome to the old man's ritual. "Yeah, Dad. Tell us about the fog."

"Well… see things sometimes."

"Like what?" Joy said.

He slurped again at the bitters. "Usually, whatever you want to see. At least that's my experience. It's like a mirror, tells a story."

"So, what do you see?" Joy asked.

"Not about what I see. It's about what you see."

"I see an old man," Rich said.

Senior laughed and nearly spilled his drink. "Well played, Son, well played. Alright. Let me get situated here. My back is killing me. I'm telling ya, that surgeon was a hack."

"He said your images were great," Helen said.

"Yeah, and then they ask me to come back next week and the week after that and… if the images are so great," he grunted and set the drink down, pulling out an orange plastic bottle of pills from his jacket pocket, "why do I still need these things?"

Joy quickly looked down and away.

"Thought you tapered off those, Dad?" Rich said, solemn.

"Did you hear what I just said?"

"Mixing is dangerous though," Joy said.

Senior shrugged in disgust. "I appreciate your concern but, quite frankly, that's your problem. Both of yours. Not mine. Doctor said to stay on schedule. So, I'm staying on schedule. Okay?"

"Fair enough," Rich said.

"Should be taking two or three, that's what I should be doing. Get in front of the pain, not behind it." He twisted open the top and tilted the bottle; a lone pill dropped onto the palm of his hand. He picked up his drink and swallowed the pill; a small exhale of relief as he set down the bottle of pills next to my Perrier. "Joy, you go first. What do you see?"

"Yes, Joy. What do you see?" Helen said, gently massaging Senior's shoulders.

Joy paused and squinted in discernment as she always did when trying to figure things out. Though she had been raised in Dover, she had never been close with the Turley family outside of her relationship to me. I could tell that a part of her was still trying to read the room. It had been a long time since I had seen that look; curious and engaged, humble, in the moment, a little vulnerable. It was a far cry from the last time I had seen her, when she more resembled the look of a wild animal ogling its next meal. I wondered if perhaps Senior and Helen held suspicions about Rich's newfound, tattered and tattooed love interest.

"Love and kindness," she said, somewhat timid. "I see love and kindness."

There was an awkward silence.

Then.

“Love and kindness,” Senior said. “Love and kindness!” Yes, I see that. Right there. The way the fog plays with the glass. Soft and easy.” He looked over his shoulder to Helen. “The way love should be. That’s nice, Joy. Really nice. Beautiful.” He sipped more of his bitter drink. “Son?”

“Yeah,” Rich said contemplative, clearly taken by Joy’s vision. He pulled her in close. “I see love and kindness, too. And you’re right, Dad, it is beautiful.”

“Oh god,” Helen said. “Nothing worse than new looovvve.”

Joy and Rich both blushed. My stomach groaned.

“Jimmy, Jesus. Get some of those bubbles down,” Senior said.

I picked up the bottle of Perrier, now with a slight sweat. The edge of the napkin brushed up against the bottle of pills causing it to fall over and twirl on top of the glass table. I quickly set down the bottle of Perrier. It made a loud clank. “I’m sorry.” I said, as I reached for the bottle of pills. My hand trembled. Senior grabbed my wrist, “Jimmy, you okay?” With his other hand, he snatched the bottle of pills, stopped the spinning, and set them straight on top of the table.

“This is ridiculous,” Rich said. “You need some food.” He stood up and shot me a concerned look that said, “Dude, I told you! You’re detoxing from the Ativan.” He went to the bar.

“No, no. That’s okay,” I said, mortified, knowing I wasn’t going to be able to keep any food down. My nerves were not hungry, they were insane.

“Don’t eat now, we have a big meal coming,” Helen said.

“And it’s going to be delicious, too!” Senior added.

“What’s for dinner?” I asked, trying to shift the focus onto anything other than me.

"Mutton," Senior deadpanned sarcastic.

"Not just mutton. Mutton chops!" Helen said.

"Served bloody—"

"Served rare," Helen corrected him. "With a wine reduction, fresh mint, lemon potatoes and roasted vegetables."

"A perfect Fall meal," Joy said.

Rich came back to the couch with two Perrier's, one for himself, one for Joy, and a small container of Planters mixed nuts. He set down the container of nuts next to the bottle of pills. To appease his concern, I attempted to eat. It was stupid of me to push it that far, to be so out of body, out of mind, so willful that I couldn't or wouldn't ask for what was clearly needed; worse, to not even know, to invert, to lean into the hunger as if it were not starvation but rather high-octane fuel ready to burn.

"How long have you been sober now, Jimmy?" Senior asked. "Twenty years, is that right?"

"Twenty-two," Joy said. "Or did you relapse?"

Joy, the queen of relapse, questioning my sobriety. Donny probably told her I relapsed on the way out. *But I didn't—did I, Lord? Relapse? I was just taking care of my dislocated jaw, right? And the counting? Doctor's orders?*

The irony snapped me into focus.

"Yes… twenty-two."

"That's a good number," Senior said. "It represents a new birth, completion of a cycle. Must be why you're here. Can you see that in the fog?"

I laughed clumsily. "No. I don't see anything in the fog."

"And no slip ups the entire time?" Helen asked.

"No slip-ups," I said firmly, the words dry as the salted Brazil nut that I was trying to swallow.

Helen seemed surprised. "Not one?"

"He just said, no slip-ups," Rich said. "Why would you even ask that? Twenty-two years. Dude's a warrior. Spiritual warrior."

"It's not personal. Just seems like I never meet anyone that's stayed sober that long. Certainly not at the Compound or the Flats."

"Why do you always have to dig?" Rich asked. "Compound is for newcomers. Flats… is the Flats. Not gonna change overnight. You know that."

"So you've said," Helen quickly replied. "But that is where we're investing. Heavily, I might add. A lot depends on the success of The Flats. You know that."

"I do know that, but what are we talking about here? You do recognize it takes time to get time, right? Building, rebuilding a community. It's not a proper comparison."

"What is a proper comparison?"

"There isn't one. Why do you think they're giving us all the jack?"

"To deliver results. Get these people off the street."

"I don't drink much anymore either," Senior said, taking a loud sip of his Bourbon and Blood. It worked, released the tension. Everyone laughed.

"California sober, right, hon?" Helen said.

"Hey, I'm no angel."

"Don't want one, either."

"Can't trust 'em, can you, darling?"

"Not one bit." Helen feigned a kiss, and Senior received it with reciprocal warmth.

"Oh Goooddd. Now who's talking about love?" Rich said.

"I think it's beautiful," Joy said blushing.

"So, Jimmy," Senior's tone turned serious. "Tell us what you see in the fog?"

I shook my head, No.

"Oh, come on," Joy said. "You always see something."

"Yeah, Jimmy. That's what you do," Rich said. "What do you see?"

It again grew quiet. Each movement—my hands, my fingers, my breath—hyper aware. All these years later and, yet still, I felt like the mono-syllabic kid in the corner thinking about himself too much; unable or unwilling, too in-between to articulate my thoughts—there are so many of them—without dissertation or a microphone, a stage, something to separate, to buffer and make sense of the distance I feel inside. Strange how when around old friends and family we revert to being a child in a matter of minutes. Perhaps it reveals more of the true self. I looked into the fog rushing fast and hard into the paned glass. What I saw was Fairview. What I said was, "Donny. I see Donny surfing Retributions."

"Oh, now that's interesting," Senior said wide-eyed, looking to Rich.

"What did he do?"

"Rich?" Helen said.

Rich scratched his forehead as if embarrassed, "I was gonna tell you later. It's what I was dealing with earlier. It's no big deal, really."

"Stealing a bus is no big deal?" Senior said.

"What, like a recovery home van?"

"No," Rich grinned, almost embarrassed. "We have a tour bus for my speaking gigs. It's big, it's nice. A Prevost."

"Gotta hand it to him. He thinks big," Senior said.

"What is it with these people and stealing?" Helen said.

"These people?" Rich said.

"No, seriously, who steals a bus?"

Donny.

My stomach burned in anger and embarrassment. It shouldn't have—he wasn't my responsibility—but it did.

"He's just detoxing," Joy said. "It's not who he is, not what's in his heart."

Yes, it is.

"I guess I am going to have a drink," Helen said. "Hon, you want a refill?"

Senior shook his head, No.

Helen walked to the bar.

"Where is he now?" I asked.

"Sleeping. Hopefully."

"He wants to be sober. I know he does," Joy said.

"No, he doesn't," Rich and I said, almost simultaneous.

"Did you talk to him?" I asked Rich.

"No, he was out of control. They gave him a sedative. A strong one, too."

"I'm sorry. I should have—"

"Should've what? There's nothing you can do. He's not the first newcomer that's stole something or tried to bounce. It's kind of how it works."

"Well, if it's how it works, like you say," Helen said from the bar. "Then we might need a hard reconsider on our allocations."

"It's a euphemism, Helen. Relax."

"I am relaxed," she said, opening a bottle of wine.

"What does he want?" Senior asked.

"*What does he want*?" Rich said, defensive.

"Everyone wants something. What does he want?"

"He wants what everyone wants."

"And what's that?"

"He wants love," Joy said.

"Exactly. Exactly! Thanks babe. A feeling of peace in his heart. Security. He wants to be needed." Rich put his arm around Joy. "Like we all do."

Joy again blushed and put her head on his shoulder.

"Please," Senior quipped. "Jimmy, what does he really want?"

I shook my head, reluctant.

"No, no, no. You've been quiet long enough now," he pressed on. "You're with family. You have twenty-two years. What does he want? Really. What does he really want?"

"Well, he wants a silver bullet. An answer to where it all went wrong, the one trauma."

"That's not true," Joy said.

"Trauma!" Senior raised his voice. "That word again!"

"He fixes that, he fixes himself. Problems go away. Only they don't go away. They just reappear in a different form."

"So, fool's gold. A mirage."

"Not a mirage, Dad," Rich said. "It's complicated. He's complicated."

"I'm complicated, too. You're complicated. We're all complicated. Great. What's it all mean, Jimmy? You got twenty-two years, tell it to me straight."

"It means… Deep down Joy and Rich are right. It is what we all want. Love, security. But what Donny wants right now is what every addict wants, a quick fix. And any fix will do as long as it doesn't involve any heavy lifting on his part."

"A gutter with a view," Rich said, listening intently.

"Yes. Lot of ego, lot of sloth. No difference."

"That's harsh," Joy said.

"Addiction is harsh," I said.

"So, recovery should be harsh?"

"No. Recovery is hard; not harsh. There is a difference."

"Well, I didn't get that from him at all," Joy said. "And I think he is different. He's special. Can't treat him like everyone else."

"Joy's right. He is special. We have to meet him where he is."

Can't see what we are can we, Lord? No. No one can. And what could I say? They were both newcomers; Joy more so than Rich, obviously, but both were locked in the struggle of wanting to be special, to make their life, their recovery, count for something more than just going to meetings for the rest of their lives. And how could they escape it? They couldn't. The hardwire. The Science of being New. The justifications and fixes for their lives. Rich building a new model army of recovery. Joy bypassing 99% of all newcomers of her street-laden ilk straight to designer suits and indescribable wealth; it requires belief and hope, dedication and commitment; and above all, a healthy dose of delusion.

Joy's anger was palpable as was, now, my own. Not that it was ever really that far, just a trudging flicker, a pilot light of disappointment. And I'm sure she was none too happy to have seen me arrive in Dover. I was the only person in that room who knew who she was, what she had done, and what she had lost.

We resent what we see only when it's what we are. And I knew that. There. Then. And always: The In Between.

Was I resentful?

Yes. Yes, I was.

But despite my obvious handicaps, I had developed some hard skills in recovery. I had learned how to play nice with others in the sandbox. What did I learn? Don't have anything nice to say, don't fucking say it. That's Science. That's Truth. That said, I seriously began to question who wrote that note.

"It's just what I've seen," I said. "You may be right."

"Where do you think he was gonna go?" Rich asked.

"San Francisco."

"Sell the bus, live in the 'loin?"

I nodded, Yes.

"Makes sense to me," Senior said. "Everything changed after San Francisco. If there's one trauma, that's the one in my book. Maybe that's why he's here. Maybe that's why we're all here." He looked to Rich. His lip trembled. "It may have taken twenty-two years but here we are, we survived. It's our time now. The stars have aligned. They always do eventually. That's Science. Let's do something with it." He raised his glass for a toast. "To A Return to Dover, a return to our promise, and our purpose."

"Here, here," Helen said, returning from the bar with an oversized glass of dark red wine.

"Couldn't have done it without you, Dad. I love you."

"Beautiful," Joy said. "Love you, Dad."

Love you, Dad? *Jesus, Lord.*

We raised our drinks and tapped the air.

Helen kissed Senior's forehead and, again, sat down at his side. "I have a question, this whole sobriety and Donny thing. Does intent even matter?"

"No," Rich said quickly, a loving glance to Joy. "It's what you do, not what you think."

"Jimmy, you agree with that?" Helen asked.

"Mostly, yeah."

"But?"

"It doesn't really matter what I think."

"Exactly," Joy said.

"Joy?" Rich said, surprised by her emotion.

"I'm just… I just mean we, *I*, don't know everything. I'm sorry, I just love Donny," her voice broke with emotion, "I think he wants to get clean."

Helen seemed to enjoy the back and forth. Again, to me, "So, you do think intent matters? I ask because it seems like it would."

"Cuts both ways. On one hand, no. Whatever gets you in the door. But that's just surface; it only lasts so long. People that I've seen stay sober long term, when they were new, had intent. They may not have been aware of it, or even acted like it, but, when the push came to shove, the intent was there. They take the difficult action; whatever that ends up being. The outer matches the inner."

"In other words, they don't steal buses," Senior said.

"You can't see intent, though," Joy said. "People make mistakes."

"She's right. Maybe you're too close," Rich said.

"I am too close. It's why I didn't want to go with him in the first place."

"Why did you?" Helen asked.

"I caved. Needed money."

"How is that caving?"

"It's not," Senior said, gently massaging Helen's thin leg in reassurance. "He did what he had to do; he helped a friend. There's nothing wrong with that. I'm tired of everyone trying to vilify money. It's ignorant."

"It's disgusting," Helen said while sipping her wine, and staring at me through the glass. "So, intent aside, do you believe in God? Is that how you stay sober? God?"

"What kind of question is that? He's sober twenty-two years. Of course, he believes in God."

"It's just a question, Rich," Senior said.

"It's inappropriate."

"No, it isn't. We're putting a lot of money into this, into you. A Return to Dover. A lot."

"And I'm grateful… I'm also working my ass off."

"Agreed."

"And?"

"And if we're going to be successful, we're going to need more success stories. Simple Science."

"We have success stories. All over. Compound. The Flats."

"Yes, but not twenty-two-year success stories. We need to hear from someone who has done it long term. Last thing we want is the Turley brand associated with some hack recovery outfit. Too much risk."

A pall fell over both Joy and Rich's face.

Rich's voice elevated. "First of all, we're not some hack recovery outfit. Second, I thought this was just going to be dinner. Jimmy's our guest, not a prospective client."

"Take it easy, Son," Senior said. "We're family here."

"Yeah. You say so."

"She's just asking a question. And it's a fair one. I want to know, too, how it works, the God thing; how it compares to The Science. Never worked for me but things have changed; might be able to help more people, especially in the Flats. That would be good for us, for A Return to Dover. Yes?"

"Yes, of course."

"What is going on in the Flats?" I asked, taking advantage of a window out of the God question.

"Right now? Shit show," Senior said.

"Thanks to Prop 1111," Helen said. "And the State of California. Decriminalize drugs. What did they think was going to happen?"

"They didn't think," Senior said. "They just reacted."

"That, and then there's the NIMBYs."

"Helen, you're a NIMBY," Rich said.

"No, I'm a taxpayer who worked her ass off and doesn't want people in psychosis dropping by for visits. They should put them all in Fairview. That's what it's there for." She looked to me. "No offense, but it's always blame the rich for everything around here."

"Yeah, until it's time to make the donor calls," Senior said. "You know, Jimmy, we used to donate as Anonymous—"

"Yes, we did," Helen said, self-satisfied.

"It was a badge of honor. We didn't need credit for doing the right thing. Now we have to sing it to the mountaintops, get out in front of it before some college kid, some professor—Jimmy, you probably know this—trying to get published, comes looking to tear it all down." He pointed to his chest. "Tear down what I built!"

"What we built," Helen said. She drank more wine and lovingly messed with Senior's long hair.

"Like I said," he cleared his throat. "What we built."

"We'll fix it, Dad. You'll see. It's an opportunity. A power shift. A way of thinking. We're getting there."

"Jimmy, how is your mom?" Senior asked. "Is she doing okay?"

"Yeah, how is your mom?" Joy asked.

"She's doing great, thanks," I said.

"Yeah, we just went and visited her," Rich said. "She looks exactly the same. You can see why Jimmy looks so young."

"Good. Good. I always liked your mom," Senior said, slurping on more of the Bourbon and Blood. "She was a good woman."

"Is a good woman," Rich said.

"Exactly. Like I said. Your dad, too. He was a good man."

I was grateful to Rich for the deflection. He didn't have to do that but, clearly, he knew that when people ask how you are, how your family is, they don't really want to know; they just want you to know that they know how important it is to ask.

Joy, on the other hand, knew that I had stopped visiting my mother long ago, yet she again decided to turn the screw. Maybe she couldn't control it, the self-hatred. I couldn't control my anger at that stage of recovery, let alone the self-hatred. Nonetheless, it was low, and my stomach soured with contempt. Just because there is a justification for being angry or nasty doesn't mean we get to spray toxicity with impunity. No. There are real life consequences for our dis-ease. Same as it ever was. No difference. There was a time and that time is gone. She was now with Rich. And it was good. And in that moment it became unconscionably clear that the longer I stayed in Dover, Fairview always within plain sight, the more impossible it would become to avoid the insecurities of my decision not to visit my mother; that this voice, the one that's always near, that even in silence still holds sway, would grow louder, and louDER, and LOUDER, an appalling accompaniment to the ever-present and relentless ring of tinnitus reverberating inside my skull.

"So, the Flats," I said. "A woman came with us. Rosie. She went there."

"Rosie's dead," Joy said.

"What?!" Helen was aghast.

"Yeah. I do intake in The Flats. We found her a few days ago in one of the tents."

"Rosie with the overalls?" I asked.

"Oh my," Helen said.

"Were you close?" Senior asked me.

"No. Donny may have been. Intake for what?"

"Anyone that wants the Health Act money has to enroll," Rich said.

As the well-worn feeling of numbness to the news of another addict's death began to kick in, my thoughts quickly drifted to memory: Rosie clutching my leg and calling me Daddy; me trying to wrangle free from her desperate grasp; the sound of her head banging against the cabinet inside the Chinook.

Out loud, I counted to three 3X. Embarrassed, I kept my head down, stared at the Perrier and pills on the glass table. "Does Donny know?"

"I told him the other day at the Compound," Joy said.

I felt myself grow angry. Something about the way Joy said it, so flat, so matter of fact, almost as if there were a gleam in her eye, a thrill of the life-and-death-of-it-all, the drama that so many newcomers fall prey to, a kind of survivor ego mixed with a level of concern that had not existed prior to the day of the nameless addict's death. *It's an ugly business isn't it, Lord*? Sometimes, it doesn't feel like anyone or anything is coming forth in a way that's real. "So, what is going on out there? Free for all, that it? Anything goes?" I asked.

"Pretty much," Helen said, drinking more wine.

"It's not a free for all," Rich said.

"Seems like it to me."

"We can't just take a scorch the earth approach and blunt force someone into rehab, or Fairview for that matter. Jesus, what's wrong with you?"

"Nothing's wrong with me." More with the wine.

"Well, it doesn't work that way."

"How does it work then?" I asked.

"The Health Act has a right-to-life mandate. Sobriety is not a requirement for the money. Helen knows this. She just likes to play both sides."

"Take it easy, Son," Senior said.

"No, I'm just sick of it," his face turning red. "She just pushes. It's a pilot program for fuck's sake. We facilitate, that's all. It's not perfect. Not supposed to be." He caught himself, pared back his eyelids and took a deep breath. "Sorry, Jimmy. I just get emotional about these things. The concept is to meet them where they are. Give them dignity, food and shelter, clothing, the means to survive, they'll eventually gravitate toward recovery."

"Naturally, organically," Joy added.

"Exactly. The last thing they need is someone shaming them into recovery."

"Who's shaming anyone?" Helen asked. "How is helping someone get off drugs and off the street shaming?"

"The decency helps them make good decisions," Rich continued. "Gives them time to find the desire to change."

"I guess Rosie ran out of time, then," Helen said.

"We all run out of time, babe," Senior said. "Rich is right. We can't force it. Things have changed. We have to embrace it, embrace the change. Free will is important."

"Rosie wanted to change," Joy said. "She just—"

"Wanted it to come organically?" I said.

"Thank you!" Helen said to me, another sip of wine.

I shouldn't have said it, but I did. As my discomfort and angst continued its ascent, the hypocrisy (my own) was not lost on me. Rich was right. Sobriety can't be forced. I had been saying that for as long as I could remember, yet now I was being confronted with it, face-to-face, the realities of my belief; only this wasn't AA, or at an open meeting where, just by walking through the door, people have made a decision, mostly, to attempt life, attempt recovery; this was different; this was a larger, more commercial and commodified setting where people, just by getting themselves to the Flats, were afforded the opportunity to not only live in squalor, but get paid for it.

I counted to three 3X.

“So, who gets the money, anybody?” I asked.

“Money for every homeless person,” Helen quipped.

“Not just the homeless,” Rich said calmly. “Addicts, of course. Mentally ill, too.”

“Which is 99% of the homeless,” finishing her wine, setting the glass down on the table next to the pills.

“More like 80% but… yes, clearly, there’s a lot of mental illness. There are poor people, too. Lot of elderly coming in. Nomads.”

“I love the nomads,” Joy said. “They always want to help.”

“Why the Flats though?” I asked. “There’s nothing out there.”

“There is now,” Helen said.

“Yes, there is,” Senior said. “Gonna be more, too.”

Exasperated, Rich shook his head. “Can we just not talk about business for a minute? This is a reunion, not a business meeting.”

“I agree,” Joy said, rubbing Rich’s back.

“It’s really pretty simple, Jimmy,” Senior said. “Out of sight, out of mind. This way the politicians and the big tech execs from up north don’t have to see it on their streets; they get their people elected; get to look like the good guys; we do the dirty work. We take the risk.”

“And we get paid for that risk,” Helen said.

A bell rang from the hallway.

"Otherwise, this whole thing," Senior continued. "Not just Dover, the entire California coastline, will be tech rich only. I mean, Turley has money, but… we can't compete with that kind of money."

"Not yet," Helen said, affirmed.

Senior leaned his head lovingly into Helen's chest. Odd as it may have seemed, it was clear they were good for each other. Good, bad, or indifferent, they were a team.

A bell rang again from the hallway.

"Sounds like your jeans are done," Joy said.

"Huh?"

"Your jeans. The dryer."

The note! As if on autopilot, I quickly stood up. My legs slightly wobbled. Senior pushed himself up off the couch and grabbed my arm. "Whoa! Whoa, whoa, whoa. You, okay?"

I peeled my eyes wide and tried to pull it together. "One, two, three. One, two, three. One, two, three," I said aloud. "I'm good. I'm good. I'll be right back. Will go get those jeans." My legs felt somewhat numb. I used Senior's firm grip to propel me forward. Robotic in my gait, all eyes upon me, I made my way out of the living room toward the hallway.

"Jimmy," Rich said. "You can get the jeans later."

"No, no. It's okay. I… I need to change."

"You don't need to change."

"No, I do. I need to change."

The hallway seemed a prism of light. My neck and backside were insensate, heated from the perceived thoughts of others. I didn't dare blink lest I succumb to my failing body; I just kept my eyes open like some sort of zombie. Perhaps I was. A zombie. Perhaps I was. The bell rang again. I grabbed the jeans out of the dryer and frantically searched for the note in the pocket. It wasn't there. I looked inside the dryer, and there it was underneath the lint trap, fully torn, right down the middle, in two distinct pieces.

I went into Hana's room and locked the door. I undressed and again saw myself in the mirror: naked, fearful. I put on the warmed-over jeans. They felt tight and constrictive. I squatted to stretch them out, but it was no use, they felt stiff and old. *What am I doing, Lord*? *What the fuck am I doing*? I sat down on the carpeted floor, my back against the rigid over-washed death of the paisley comforter. I pieced together the note, and my vision began to narrow.

One, two, three. One, two, three. One, two, three.

One, two, three. One, two, three. One, two, three.

One, two, three. One, two, three. One, two, three.

"You alright in there?" Rich asked.

He jostled the door handle.

"Yeah, just give me a minute."

One, two, three. One, two, three. One, two, three.

One, two, three. One, two, three. One, two, three.

One, two, three. One, two, three. One, two, three.

"Ahh, fuck man. C'mon, Jimmy. I'm sorry, I feel bad. This was a bad idea. You want to just bounce now? We can just go… get some McDonald's. Hit the road back to L.A. Be like old times."

Old times.

"You'll be home in the morning."

I looked at the note. *I wasn't going home was I, Lord*? No.

"Probably better to leave now anyways," he said. "I got this whole speaking thing coming up in Detroit and New York. Be good for me to get back to Dover early, rest up before I go. You worried about Donny? Don't worry about

Donny. He's good here. I'll put him to work. It'll be good, you'll see."

"Just give me a minute."

Almost every part of my being wanted to tell him, Yes, take me home, take me back to the Vortex. This is a bad idea. All of it. But there was nothing to go back to and, all this time, I knew it. The only thing stopping me was a grotesque lack of humility which, at twenty-two years sober, was humiliating.

I stood up.

I took off the jeans.

I put the khakis back on.

I stuffed the torn pieces of the note into my mouth.

I wouldn't lose it again.

I chewed and I swallowed.

Then, I opened the door.

"Mutton sounds good."

Prologue (3)

"Poor Cassio, what a lop, that guy," Donny would say.

This is how it would start, back in the day.

"Could argue he caused the whole thing."

"Cassio?" I asked, incredulous.

The long late-night drives on tour in the Chinook.

"Well, listen. Everyone thinks Iago sabotaged."

"That's because he did."

I would be driving.

"Right. But Cassio should've been more on guard."

"On guard for what?"

Rich would be asleep.

"His weaknesses, man. Can't be drinking and whoring when you're no good at drinking and whoring."

"Blame the weakness, that's your thesis?"

Donny would pull out his dog-eared copy of Othello.

"Dude's a lieutenant. He has a responsibility."

"And?"

To help me stay awake he would read aloud.

"What I'm saying is, you are what you are. Get off the sidelines, do your fucking job."

"He did do his job."

Then we would find a way to argue.

"Did he, though?"

"He becomes the Governor."

Sometimes about Othello.

"Kind of pithy. All that damage just to be Governor?"

"He stumbled forward. Survived. It's noble."

Sometimes about nothing at all, and it would get heated.

"I ain't buying it. Besides, he plays the whore. Leads her on. Not cool."

"Her name is Bianca," I'd lay in. "She's a courtesan. Do you even know what that is?"

I wish I could take some of that back now.

"Like I said, he plays the whore, wants the throne. Simple. No different than Iago. Stumbling. Plotting. Whatever the fuck you want to call it. No difference."

"No difference? You have lost the plot. Clearly."

I didn't have to be right. He was trying to help.

"Can't pretend like dude don't want more. He's in the game. He wants more. That's how it is. Everyone wants more."

"Is it in the text? No. Don't be dumb. If I were your teacher, you'd get an F."

I didn't have to be mean. He was trying to help.

"If you were my teacher?" He laughed. "Motherfucker, you ain't even able to finish high school."

"Able is different than want. I just didn't want to. Too much groupthink. It's bullshit."

I could have just let him have his say.

"Know that's right. Fall in line fucks. But still, if you were my teacher? Please." He paused and inhaled deeply. "Shit, I don't know. Maybe it was a writer mistake."

"A writer mistake. Shakespeare? Please."

I could have been more loving.

"Only staged a few times. Who knows what they did to the text after dude died? You don't know. You damn sure don't know."

"He didn't make mistakes, Donny. That wasn't his thing."

We were children.

"Not my thing either." He drum rolled on the dash of the Chinook. "It's why my timing is so tight! Tell ya one thing, Cassio damn sure made a mistake. Idiot is what he is."

Rest.

Chapter Three: *Bolero*

THE DAY WE LEFT DOVER, Donny got thirty days sober. He was happy to be on the road. I was, too. Felt good to look out the window again, see something, see nothing—no talking, no attachments— just hypnotic observation perfectly balanced, masterfully mixed into a personalized soundscape; the instrumentation simple: an oversized engine, cool fall air, and mountainous rubber tires smoothly rolling over endless miles of pavement; pushing forward against whatever the elements had to offer that day. The counting non-existent… felt like home.

Only we weren't home.

The long stretches of no talking were not solely due to the mindful meditation, it was also Donny's simmering resentment of not being invited to the Turley dinner; it was easier for him to blame me, lest he bite the hand that feeds. I didn't like it, but I understood it. And to be fair, I was resentful, too. Who the fuck steals a tour bus is right! It's stupid, disrespectful, a clear sign that whatever intention he had of getting sober was, at best, conditional.

I guess it always is.

Funny how it works though, the very thing he wanted just a few days ago he was now driving. This was by design.

"Have to lean into the Science, the disruption," Rich said. "This lets the newcomer discover for themselves that their way doesn't work; that it won't quell the mania. They'll no longer have anyone to blame. This is good; it will lead to a make or break. And either way, they get to own their decision."

It was hard to disagree with. I did wonder about at what cost but, ultimately, he was right; it didn't take long for the bus and the road to no longer appease Donny's dis-ease, his desire for something more.

In long term recovery, this type of experience is usually a bellwether for knowing precisely when the problem is oneself. But for the newcomer, the bell has been cracked for so long that its incessant clang falls on deaf ears, it signifies nothing; for the lead sheep is not only castrated, it is also deranged.

We recover one day at a time, yes. But it takes years if not decades to unwind the need-it-now wiring. Sometimes never. This is why you hear people say it's a miracle.

Because it is.

Donny's job was to drive; my job was to advance the shows; twenty-two of them. Felt weird to call it that, a show, but that is what it was. One-thousand people would be in attendance in Detroit; five thousand in New York. *Five thousand, Lord*! Bigger than any show The In Between ever did, that's for sure. It was impressive. I wondered how Rich must feel fronting that kind of performance, to remember all those words. I mean, I did a lot of nervy gigs back in the day, opening for bands I had idolized, wanting to be great, to show them I belonged. But to be alone, acapella, nothing to smooth over the imperfections, the mistakes, had to have been nerve wrecking. Not that he showed it. I imagined his experiences in prison made whatever fears he had seem insignificant, child's play.

Advancing the shows was a bit like being a tour manager, only instead of calling on production managers and promo people, hotels, venue security staff, and management, I called non-profits and ministers of various churches and self-help organizations, some using AA's twelve steps directly, most using some variation thereof—Christ, harm reduction, suboxone, lithium, lots and lots of lithium—to provide structure, to house and help the homeless, the mentally ill, and drug addicted get on their feet.

My only edict from Rich was to never discuss or accept money. And that was fine by me; it helped to ease my concerns of all the AA appropriation, of profiting from something that I, to ensure continued sobriety, should be doing for free: helping others.

The bus itself was a top-of-the-line split-level Prevost filled with satellite TVs, laptops, a front and rear lounge, espresso machines, top and bottom, refrigerators filled with organic food and drink. Each bunk, of which there were twelve, had climate-controlled HEPA filtered AC along with a mini-TV screen that dropped from the panel above; electrical outlets to charge any devices; two prong adapters for three prong foreign travel. The thing had it all. I was given an iPhone (as was Donny) to conduct business and I spent much of my time on the road reacquainting myself with the user interface. I'd had an early version back in the day, so there was some familiarity, but it was a big learning curve, no doubt. It was also addictive. Why talk to someone? Why ask a question when you can just figure it out yourself?

Rich and Joy shared the top level of the bus, and for the most part kept to themselves. Joy avoided me like the plague. She'd come down for appearances, say hello, talk with

Donny; this, mostly, when Rich and I needed to discuss anything related to the shows. Strangely, I didn't mind. What were we going to do, talk about the old times? No. The road helped. But it wasn't just the road. Being around her calmed a part of my nervous system, my spirit, that for years had been more or less in constant agitation. Seeing her in person, not in my imagination, not dead in some encampment, or strung out, or raped, or selling herself to whomever was holding, all the real, daily occurrences of life on the street; seeing her thrive in sobriety; it gave me hope that by staying clean myself, maybe I had some part in not just her destruction—it takes two, and I know I was not easy to live with—but also her recovery. *I don't know, Lord.* Seems silly. But whatever it was, with her around, felt like I could breathe.

***

Saturday. Mid-morning. We pulled into the Cass Corridor a few miles outside of downtown Detroit. It was sunny and surprisingly warm for early November. Billowing white and pink clouds pooled above. I rolled down the window. A thick and humid air attached itself to my skin.

"Damn, look at this shit," Donny said. "Tapas, wine bar. Lofts. Where's all the whores?"

"Jesus, Donny. Whores?"

"You know what I mean. Gentrification, man. It's fucking everywhere. No authenticity no more, nowhere."

"You realize you lived in Venice, right? It's basically the gentrification capital of the world. No whores there."

"Actually, there are."

"No there isn't. Homeless whores?"

"Don't judge; still got hustle."

Bemused, if irritated, I started laughing. "So, let me get this straight. You're out there, living in the canals with all the million-dollar homes, venture capitalist girlfriend."

"Partner."

"Partner. Hitting all the overpriced thrift stores, doing the homeless chic thing. Keeping it real with the dirty used shoes."

He laughed. "Gotta stop the sweat factories."

"Drinking ten-dollar local lattes, getting your ass bleached. That how it works?"

"Hey man, don't knock it 'til you try it."

"Okay, fair. But you don't really think those rich people are locals, do you?"

"Some of 'em are."

"Please. They're grifters."

"Just 'cause I got style don't mean I'm wrong."

"Actually, I think it does."

"Eh, that's 'cause you're white."

"Back to that, huh?"

"What?"

"That's the second time you've said that. Why would you say that?"

"'Cause you are! You wouldn't understand. You always had a choice."

"That's a pretty selective memory you have. Your family lived in the Heights. We were in the tenements."

"Still had choice."

"Yeah, choice between me and Dad and who would pull out the blue roll of food stamps and start counting in line. Choice between color of used Huskies."

He laughed. "Fucking Toughskins. That shit's funny."

"Didn't seem too funny to me."

"Alright, alright. Why you always gotta get serious and shit? Just fucking with ya."

"Yeah, you said that before, too. It's bullshit. You got something to say, fucking say it."

"Take it easy, Jesus. Just talking shit."

"Yeah, you say so."

"Yeah, I say so."

We drove deeper into the Cass Corridor. Donny was right about one thing, the area had changed; looked a lot safer now than what I had remembered; a lot safer than the Vortex, that's for sure, most of L.A. proper for that matter.

"Dude, we played around here. Remember?"

"No."

I did. I just didn't want to go down punk rock memory lane again. If I did, it would never end; for Donny, memory was like taking a drink, one was too many and one hundred was not enough; I learned this the hard way; story after story, glorifying a way of life that no longer exists: decadence, depravity, vice as virtue. Every cliche the world has now been forced to smear onto the musician life (this mostly due to the musicians themselves selling tell-all books, making it a brand, a reality TV show, a podcast, a dirty little window for the voyeur to walk through unencumbered by shame or guilt, "Hey, look at all my degradation").

Made me ill.

We don't do yesterday do we, Lord? No. There was a time and that time is gone. We do today. Here, now. Nothing else matters.

Nothing.

"You don't remember? We slayed it that night, hooked up with those black punk chicks, went back to their place. The boyfriends came knocking, fucking dude put the gun to your head. I know you remember that."

"I remember."

"Well, why didn't you say so, shit! Those were good times."

"Good times? Nearly shat myself."

"You didn't act like it. You were cool as a cucumber."

"Just a defense."

"Defense of what?"

"I just told you. How afraid I was. Can't let them in, let them see you. That whole thing, Dad taught me that. I don't live like that anymore."

"Ya kind of do though."

"I think I've been pretty straight with you."

"Maybe your dad was right. Saved your life."

"Yeah, saved it and took it."

"No difference."

"Right. It's zero sum; not a way to live."

"I don't know, dude. At least we were in the game."

"What game is that?"

"Game of life, bro. Gotta take life. Can't sit around and wait for it to happen. That's not what we do. We're fucking rockers, man. In our hearts, remember? Way of life. Thin fucking Lizzy," He started singing. "I am your main man if you're looking for trouble / I take no lip, no one's tougher than me."

"Oh my god."

"I know you love this song. Come on… 'I'd kick your face, you'd soon be seeing double / Hey, little girl, keep your hands off of me / I'm a rocker / I'm a roller too, baby.' He reached for his iPhone on the expansive tech-burdened dash. "I gotta find that song right now."

"Just watch the road."

"Please." Fumbling for phone. Lane creep.

"Watch the fucking road!"

"No. No, man. Doctor is in the house. You need this. It'll help you remember where you're from, ya fuck. Show some respect, too."

"Respect. Stealing a bus, that's respectful."

"Just got tight. Take it easy."

"Why you so concerned with the way I live, what I need? Why don't you just worry about the way you live? Try that."

"Deny the past, deny the present. Isn't that what the man says?"

Rich opened the curtain and entered the driver cabin. "Morning gentlemen. What does the man say?"

Donny quickly set the phone down. "Deny the past is to deny the present. That right?"

"Sounds about right to me." Rich gently put his thick tattooed hand on top of Donny's shoulder, a cup of coffee in the other. "Good job getting us here."

"See!" Donny said to me, emphatic. "Least someone appreciates my shit."

Rich grinned. He looked fresh and alive, black Turley sweats and hoodie, ready to start the day. "You two getting sick of each other already?"

"Pssshit," Donny said. "Dude over here thinks he needs to help people, but he's the one who needs help."

"Is that the church up there on the corner, with the steeple?" Rich asked.

"That's it," I said. "The Pastor said we could park it on the street, just past the parking lot."

"What's with all the fucking bike lanes?" Donny said. "Take a whole lane away. And for what?"

"The environment," Rich said.

"Please. I bet you there's like three tech-ass white people that use this shit bike lane on-the-reg."

"Still better for the environment," Rich quipped. "Look there's the Old Miami, where we played."

"What, where?" Donny's head turned on a swivel.

"Watch the road!" I said.

Donny pressed hard on the brakes.

Rich spilled his coffee.

"Shit! Sorry, dude."

"All good," Rich said, shaking his head as if the day were off to a dubious beginning. "We'll go check it out later."

Check it out later? *Jesus, Lord. Now what?*

"There's a spot," I said. "See that? Right in front of those lane dividers."

Outside of the church there was a line of people, hundreds, extending around the block, waiting for the mobile medical clinic inside the church parking lot to open the gates.

Donny parked the bus.

"Okay, quick check in for the day," Rich said. "Joy's not feeling well, so it'll just be us today."

"She alright?" I asked.

"Yeah, she's just… tired, I think. I don't know. Probably from all the weather changes. She wants to rest and be ready for New York."

"I'm tired too, man," Donny said. "Gotta get some sleep."

"Yeah, that's a good idea. Do it. Take care of yourself," Rich said. "I'll be in the mobile clinic most of the morning, but I want to keep the afternoon loose. Jimmy, will you talk to the pastor, see if I can speak in the parking lot instead of the church? Feels like an outside day."

"Sure. I'm supposed to meet her at 9am."

"Great. Assuming that's okay with her, we'll do lunch and then I'll speak, sign some books, then we can bounce for

New York. If not, we'll just stick to the same old, same old. No need to push her on it, okay?"

"What about the Old Miami?" Donny asked.

"Oh, yeah, we can do that," Rich replied quickly, an air of distraction. "I mean, I want to see how Joy's doing, but as long as we can be in Long Island by noon tomorrow, we're good."

"Speed drive. Coffee up. No problem!"

"Okay, cool. Give me 10 minutes. I'm gonna go check in with Joy first, let her know what's up, then we'll get to it."

Rich left the cabin. There was an awkward silence. As we gathered our belongings, a few stragglers waiting in line for the mobile clinic to open approached the bus. One of them, a dark-haired young man, twenty-something, maybe, handsome if emaciated, held a skateboard in his hand and wore an old Turley "T" t-shirt, Gutter Punk edition, crayon style, along with a pair of dark green skinny jeans and dirty white Chucks. The sleeves of the Turley t-shirt were cut off and with a Sharpie the image of the Turley "T" had been altered into an anarchy symbol. Using the bus as a mirror, he picked at the pimples on his face. The other two, a couple in their late 40s, came to the front window. "Hi! Hello!" The man shouted. "We came from Waukegan. We're here for The Science. Is Rich in there? We wanted to say hello and thank him for all he's done."

I avoided eye contact and cooly waved so as to not infer any forthcoming special treatment. Never know what the other person deduces from eye contact. Harsh? Yes. But I learned this the hard way, not only from my time on the streets as a junkie punk squatter kid fending off grifters and sex offenders, but also as a professor. Niceties and eye contact can infer a bond, and with that comes an expectation. Conversely, it can also infer aggression. Better to be honest.

You don't know me, I don't know you. Trust is earned. I nodded to the bus door, that we'd be coming out soon.

Donny shook his head in disappointment. "It's gonna be a long day."

"We'll be alright," I said. "Go get some sleep."

"Line looks nasty."

"Could be worse; could be us in that line."

"Shit, I'd rather be dead than caught in that line."

His forgetfulness of where he had come from a mere 30 days ago angered me, that and the clear lack of humility. "So much for your gentrification concerns."

"Man, you need to get up off me… before this shit gets serious." He grabbed his backpack and phone and stormed out of the cabin.

I shouldn't have said it, Lord.

The hypocrisy was killing me.

***

One of the enduring challenges of long term sobriety is knowing where all the trap doors are yet still being unable to prevent people from falling into those very same traps. This is because with the newly recovering addict, self-deception and hypocrisy reign supreme. We can talk ourselves blue—logos, pathos, ethos—literally shake the person we're trying to help out of their egoist and woe-is-me stupor; get them to see the underlying false narrative they use like an addict (there is no difference) to justify their movement toward self, always self, only to succumb to the futility of it all. Because in the end the synaptic hardwire choice will always lean into destruction. This is Science. This is Truth.

So, mostly, I learned to remain silent and take whatever feeble stab I could at transforming the energy of frustration and judgment to that of acceptance; to live and let live; to ultimately, hopefully, love.

Always back to love.

It's not easy.

There is a reason why people do not stay sober long term. As the years roll by, a dogged sense of isolation grows in tandem with recovery. People begin to look at you differently, as if somehow you, having been sober for so long, were above it all and had no problems, no frustrations of your own. The irony abounds, for not only do you feel more fragile, more frustrated, but you also feel more alone. Ninety-five percent of the people I got sober with, broke bread with, exchanged phone numbers with, are now dead; that's if they were lucky.

Because sometimes, we don't die.

We live.

We endure. Alive and high out on the street, drinking and drugging, dragging people, anyone will do, down, terrorizing our beleaguered and bewildered family members, our determined and well-meaning friends.

It can get ugly.

Much uglier than death.

And, yes, there are those people in recovery who revel in the perceived superiority of being the popular know-it-all elder. They are never alone and yet somehow, if you look close enough—it's in the eyes—always alone.

That never worked for me, not really; made me feel small and constricted, disconnected to purpose. And the few times that I did dip in, I was startled by its power and the ease with which I could get my way. A clear threat to sobriety.

So, yes, I erred toward isolation. In many ways, I was built for it, my Serbian Science, an endless fascination with thought life, my ponderings a match for silence and confinement. Sucks sometimes. And I don't blame my father or mother for my Science. How could I when I love it so, when I refuse to let it go? There is always a way through. It's just never easy, not in The In Between.

I was relieved to not have to deal with Joy for the day. It wasn't just that she was with Rich, though that did creep around some of my more sensitive edges; me wondering (knowing) what they were doing on the top level of the bus; wondering why she wouldn't have come back to me after gaining some sobriety or even make amends for all the madness she put me through during her active addiction. What was it that Rich had that I did not have? *Not a great question is it, Lord*? No. And it wasn't just the constant exposure to her physical being, seeing what she had done to her face, her body, the plastic and Botox, the tattoos, all the attempts to wash away the scars of the street, the heart. No. It was being witness to her fight, her struggle, against what I viewed as the regality, the honor and the beauty of the aging process.

Let it all drop, babe.

You're beautiful.

Immaculate.

I know, Lord. She wasn't the only one. Seems like most all of the women my age had, one way or another, taken to the knife. There are reasons. Nevertheless, it made my stomach sour, and my heart collapse a little further into itself. There is nothing like a woman in full acceptance of herself: body, mind, spirit. It's a powerful thing.

I wish I was better than that kind of judgment.

I just didn't know how to bridge the gap, to speak freely with her. I felt stifled by contempt and respect for what we once had; reverence for Rich who was able to help bring her to a new life. And yes, the thought occurred to me to make a move, a full-frontal declaration of my love. Perhaps that is what she wanted. Perhaps that is why she was so hostile to my presence. Because I didn't do that.

That it? A simple jealousy? Or was it just a plain old ordinary science: too many damn holes in the vessel, too much water onboard, and this the price paid.

***

I went into the galley to grab a couple energy bars from the refrigerator. Donny was right, it was going to be a long day, and I wasn't much for the soup kitchen food. Sometimes it was good, but not on a regular basis; the starch and sodium tore up my increasingly sensitive stomach.

Donny re-entered the galley in cut-off jean shorts, high to the groin, and an old black and white In Between t-shirt. In one hand he held a backpack, the other a Turley skateboard. Rich had the board special made for Donny getting thirty days sober. The underside was an air-brushed collage of The In Between photos and flyers that Donny had hung on the walls inside the Chinook.

"Not gonna sleep?" I asked.

He brushed past me, didn't respond.

"Look, I'm sorry. I shouldn't have said that."

"What?"

"I'm sorry. I shouldn't have—"

"Jimmy Marsan says he was wrong?"

"I didn't say I was wrong."

"Why would you apologize then?"

"Don't have anything good to say, don't say it. I shouldn't have said it."

"So, it was wrong."

I almost did it. Right there, kept the argument alive. My desire to be right, still working hard all these years later. It's always the how and when more than the what, our words, the importance we place on them. Strange that we care so much about words, that we are so sensitive to them, and yet we refuse to build the linguistic muscles required to fend off the said offenders without resorting to the very violence we abhor.

There is a reason we call it Language Arts. There is also a reason no one learns the art: violence is exciting, and easy, and you can make more money doing it.

A lot more.

"You're right," I managed to say. "I'm just tired. Too much time on the road."

"Pssshhh," he said with a droll, resigned smile. "Couple of bickering old bitches," he put his fist up for a bump, "same as it ever was?"

"Same as it ever was."

Rich came down the spiral stairs.

"Just gotta shake off the road," Donny said preemptive, putting the backpack over his shoulders.

Rich nodded in affirmation. "Alright then. Remember, we get out there, we're ambassadors of Turley, A Return to Dover. We're here to help." He gave us each reassuring eye contact. "You ready? Let's do this."

The bus doors opened. The clatter of voices from the people standing in line went silent. That him? Dude with the Science? He the man? One with the money? With a stiff upper lip, a mix of disgust and contempt, the kid popping the pimples approached Rich. "You the ones with the subs and the Narcan?"

Donny quickly stood in front of Rich and tilted his head. "Fuck you say?" The aggressive stance drew the attention of the people standing in line, eyeballs widened, incognito glares. The couple asking about Rich quickly withdrew back into the line, fearful of escalation.

Rich put his hand on Donny's shoulder and softly moved him to the side then asked the kid, "Are you here for the subs?"

"Nope."

"Just cruising?"

"Yep."

"I like what you did with the Turley shirt. It's cool."

The kid looked down at his shirt, shrugged.

"Looks like you've been going at your face pretty hard. I used to do that. You alright?"

"Is The Siren in there?" the kid asked, his voice now soft, a bit elevated.

"The Siren?"

"The Siren UK. They in there? That why you're here?"

"No," Donny said, flat.

Rich looked questioningly to Donny.

"It's a band," Donny said.

"Cool. They any good?" Rich asked.

"They're alright."

Rich's head tilted back. "Ahhh, I see. You thought we were them," he said to the kid.

"Nooo!" the kid said uncomfortable, awkward.

"It's an all-girl band," Donny said.

"They don't identify gender," the kid said quick, curt.

"Trust me, kid. They all have boyfriends. They're girls."

"That doesn't mean anything."

"Means it's bullshit, kid. A grift. Business. Gender is business. Wake up."

"What are they like?" Rich said to the kid trying to diffuse Donny's rhetoric.

"Fire."

"Don't get carried away, been done before," Donny said to the kid. Then to Rich, "It's a three-piece thing, hardcore. But girls, so everyone thinks it's new and cool. Guitar player is alright."

"Ohhh, you thought we were the roadies," Rich said laughing at himself. "They playing across the street today, that why you're here?"

The kid nodded, Yes.

"Cool. What time they go on? Maybe we'll go."

"Three. You got any food?"

"You want money instead?" Donny asked.

"Yeah," the kid said, taking the bait.

"Donny, chill. Please. We don't have money. We do have food though. But all these people—"

"They're waiting for food, too," Donny interrupted.

"Shit. They're waiting for subs," the kid said fidgety, a crooked snarl.

The people in line held serious and sunken stares with an air of impatience. The vibe: fuck that kid, open the gates, we got things to do.

"This kid's a grift. He ain't hungry," Donny said.

"Can help me if you want," I said.

"That's a good idea," Rich said. "You want to hang out, get some food, help us out before the show?"

"What would I have to do?" the kid asked me.

"Not much," I said. "Set up some tables, unload some boxes, pass out clothes. Won't take long."

"Can get you some new Turley clothes, too," Rich said.

"I don't want new clothes."

Donny dropped the skateboard from his hand, the wheels loudly smacked the concrete. "This is stupid. Dude don't even know whose shirt he's wearing."

The kid rolled his eyes, gave Donny a dismissive smirk and, as if to prove something, gain some alpha, also dropped his skateboard onto the concrete. He rested his foot on top of the kicktail, tapped it so that the board moved up and down.

Sensing the stupidity at play and to change the direction of energy into something positive, Rich asked, "What's your name?"

"Joey."

"Joey, I'm Rich. That's Jimmy, and that's Donny. You heard of The In Between?"

"Punk band?"

"Jimmy Marsan, right there. Lead singer, guitarist. Donny Whitness, drummer."

"Yeah, and that's Rich Turley, the bass player," Donny said. "You know, the dude who made the shirt you're wearing."

"Are you playing The Old Miami?" Joey asked.

"Never know—" Donny said.

"No," I said quickly. "We're here with A Return to Dover, be of service. Have to get started though. You want to help?"

"What happened to your face?"

"Oh, damn!" Donny said with a spontaneous laugh. "Joey gonna come all hard. Happened to his face? The fuck happened to your face, Joey? Try eating a salad."

"I got stabbed," I said.

"Doesn't look like you got stabbed."

Something about the way he said it, there was an innocence, made my shoulders drop. "No, it doesn't, does it. What's it look like to you?"

"Like a stamp or something."

"He's not wrong," Donny said.

"Like a scarification thing, a brand."

"California roadkill, Joey. That's the brand," Donny said. "California roadkill."

"You play music?" I asked.

"No. I want to. My stepdad has a bass. He said I could have it but only if I practice with him every day."

"Practice is good, important."

"Practice sucks."

"Why'd you ask about the subs and the Narcan?"

"'Cause that's what they're all talking about," he pointed to the people in line. "So, like," his voice raised again, "are they in there, the Siren UK?"

"Oh, Jesus. We just told you!" Donny said.

Joey shrugged. "I heard they like to help the homeless when they're on tour."

"S-u-p-e-r-f-a-n."

"I'm not a superfan."

"Admit it, Joey. Be easier for everyone. You're a superfan."

The kid glared at Donny; face turning red.

"Fucking superfans," Donny continued. "Always first in line, always want something for nothing. We look like the fucking Siren UK to you?"

Joey kicked his board at Donny then charged him with a wild barrage of punches. Donny, at least foot taller, anticipated the attack and with little effort leaned to the side, an amused look on his face. The punches all missed. Donny jerked his shoulders, bobbed and weaved as if he were going to throw a return blow. He wasn't but Joey flinched and threw another feeble onslaught of punches that also all missed.

Face-to-face, Rich grabbed Joey by the arms. “Whoa, whoa, whoa, whoa, whoa, whoa! Take it easy. Take it easy.”

The crowd groaned.

Donny looked at me and smiled wide like it was all a big joke, another hilarious, comedic, punk rock episode.

Joey grunted and yelled, “Child abuse! Child abuse! Someone call the police!”

The people in line took videos with their cell phones.

“It’s okay. It’s okay,” Rich said. “You’re not a superfan. You’re not a superfan. We know that. Come on.” Joey continued to struggle but Rich was in total command and held firm. “Come on. Come on, let’s get you some food, get you some new clothes.”

“I told you; I don’t want your stupid clothes! Let me go!”

“I will. I will. No more punches, okay? No more punches.”

Joey said nothing.

“Okay?”

“Okay! Alright! Jesus, let me go!”

Rich let go and Joey spat in his face; his nose and eyes covered in thick, adrenaline filled saliva. Rich didn’t move. He just stood there, face and neck purple in anger (whose wouldn’t be?), staring at the concrete. The removed swastika tattoo on his neck again shone white.

Joey quickly hopped on his board to skate off the sidewalk. Donny grabbed him by the arm, “Fuck you going?” Joey punched him in the throat. Staggered, Donny lost balance and fell off the curb into the gutter. Joey took off on the skateboard, pushing hard and fast toward the downtown skyline.

No one in line moved.

I helped Donny stand up.

"Well, that was fun," he said, angry and self-conscious. "Fun time's over fuckers! Can stop your filming now." No one stopped filming. Donny shook his head. "Fucking slaves," he yelled at them. "Now I'm gonna go skate. Film that too, ya fucks!"

"Don't go after the kid," I said.

"What?"

"Don't go after the kid."

"What are you, my fucking babysitter?"

"No, I'm your coach. Remember?"

"Yeah… that time's gone, bro. That time is gone."

I turned and looked to Rich. He had taken off his shirt and was wiping the spit from his face. His entire upper torso, bulky and defined, was covered in an assortment of bold prison tattoos and thick fibrous scars; looked like he had been whipped with a straight razor then tried to cover it up with tattoos. Through pursed lips he said, "This is why we're here."

"What, to get spit on? Please. I'm out." Donny hopped on his skateboard and took off toward the kid downtown.

Joy came out of the bus. Frantic and pale, her hair was disheveled and wild. She wore matching pink Turley sweats and looked at me like she was disgusted: What the fuck is going on here, and why aren't you doing anything about it? She stormed past me to Rich. "You okay, honey. Baby… baby, you okay?"

Rich remained motionless. Joy softly petted his broad shoulders. Still wiping at the spit, he addressed the people in line, his voice deep and booming. "People want to know how it works… this is how it works. People want to know what The Science is, when the change comes… this is what The Science is, this is when the change comes. I against I. That's how it works. I. Against. I."

"I against I," the couple said aloud in unison.

"I against I," someone else said.

Rich acknowledged the call and response. He put his arm around Joy's thin waist, leaned his forehead into hers. "It'll be alright," he whispered. "Not the first time I've been spit on." She put her hand onto his chest; the diamond engagement ring sparkled alive in the Detroit sun.

"Let me go change," he said aloud to the people in line. "We'll get that gate open. Get you taken care of." He took Joy by the hand and walked past me toward the bus. His eyes were dark and focused, glossed over red, "We're not going to The Old Miami. He's not back by three, we leave without him. Either way, you drive to New York."

Joy was visibly shaken and angry and did not, could not, would not make eye contact. The people standing in line were in awe of Rich, what he said, what he didn't say, didn't do. Their relief was palpable. The gates would soon be open. They would get their food and medicine.

I looked south. Donny glided smooth on his skateboard, back and forth like a snake, not a care in the world as he carved his way down the middle of the Cass Corridor toward downtown. The skyline was brilliant and blue. In the distance, beyond the tall reflective mirrored buildings—*of all things, Lord, a mirror*—fast
rising cumulus clouds with hues of pink, purple, flaming orange and red, as if burning from the inside, towered high above Lake Erie.

It would rain soon.

***

When I was a child in Hollywood, Dad in Vietnam, my mother and I, in between the three-day visits from her hairy-nut hippie friends, would have these talks wherein she preached compassion. I loved these talks. They would go something like this: I would cook macaroni and cheese from the box on an old beater gas stove that she used to light her cigarettes with, and, when things got low (twice that I'm aware of), stuff her head into. As the water came to boil, she, with her tall, green bottle of dark red wine, no glass, her lengthy cigarette and golden translucent ashtray filled high, would sit at our kitchen table, powder blue Formica with matching vinyl chairs, and sermonize somewhat sloppy on the virtues of compassion: "Nooo. No. No. No. They got it all wrong. That's not what it's about. Got it all wrong. It's about compassion. Compassion, compassion! Goddamned compassion! That's where it's at. Who are these people, anyway? These little people. They don't know me; they don't speak for me. What do they know about me, 'my overshoes,' about being a woman? They know nothing. That's what they know. You know what I say? I say fuck 'em. Fuck 'em all." A deep drag off her long cigarette, a gulp of wine. "Yeah, that's how you do it. That's how it's done. But you're not like them are you, Jimmy? No, you're not like them. You're different. I've known that about you since the day you were born. Dad don't know it. But I know it. I can see the look in your eye, you know it too, don't you? That's my boy."

My heart would fill over warm, just the idea, the concept, the empowerment of being called special. Of course, she didn't say the word, special; that was more my childish interpretation. I would have put up with all the hairy-nut hippies and psychotic episodes in the world for the narcotized effects of her calling me special. In fact, I can hardly think of another drug that brings forth such hope and imagination, such consistent pleasure, comfort and contentment.

But like every good drug, there is never enough. Everything is temporary as the exultation inevitably turns and gives way to its antithesis: the come down.

I'd like to think that the "talks" were helpful, that it gave me not only a feeling of being exceptional, that perhaps there was a purpose to my life, but also that my mother's concerns of compassion, *Compassion, Compassion*! as she would say, overcame her neurosis and shot right through my even then, at such a young age, steely disposition and proved there was another way to be in this life.

You never know who'll be the one to change everything. We don't shoot our wounded; and we don't shoot the messenger either.

They might just save your life.

***

6 am. The last stop on the tour was a defunct amphitheater in Long Island, New York. A series of hurricanes had rendered the venue mostly unusable, but Rich had a connection with one of the owners and thought it was the perfect place to end the tour; an east coast Sanctuary as it were, a pilgrimage for his followers from the surrounding boroughs. The call time to meet the owner of the venue and advance the show was 9 am. I pulled the bus off the highway and drove onto a dirt road for a short distance, then parked the bus in a muddy lot near the site. Joy, Rich, and Donny were still asleep. My eyes were bleary from the overnight drive. I needed sleep, but having never been to the east coast I decided to shake off the road and walk the amphitheater grounds, then go see the ocean and the famed white sands of Jones Beach. I could sleep later.

If there was a later.

Cloudy and cool with no wind; the topography was mostly marshland, ephemeral pools and sand dunes; unkempt bike paths and tattered wooden slat bridges. The air was moist and thick, filled with a heavy redolence of salt and fish from a stagnant slack tide. Pigeons cooed. Piping Plovers chirped. My mind was quiet, and peaceful; my thoughts were that of gratitude, of not only having successfully made the drive, but also for the alone time and being somewhere I had never been. Not much room in the adjunct professor budget for travel. Not much room for anything. One might think that, given everything that had transpired since the stabbing, more alone time would be the antithesis of what I needed. But being alone in the elements is not really being alone.

It's being one.

I walked across a bridge that led to the amphitheater stage. The wooden slats were creaky, splintered and sagging in the middle, and stood no more than a foot or two above the still water. In the distance, a Great White Heron walked gracefully along a grassy fringe near the water. It suddenly stopped and, with its long bill, daggered into a small pool of water, pulling out a large frog. The frog spasmed, its muscular arms and legs spread surprisingly wide. The heron could not gulp it down, so it stabbed the frog over and over and over until the frog hung lifeless from its bill.

I love herons, always have. Solitary and seemingly unphased by the corcass conditions of their habitat, their very existence is an artistic contradiction; they are like a Russian ballerina who while onstage gracefully preens and prances and delights the crowd then, when offstage, prowls the city streets and savagely stalks her prey. Outside of climate change, the heron has no real predators. Their offspring do though. Who? Who could it be? Who else? Vultures. The *Cathartidae*, lazy and nasty as they are, able yet unwilling to hunt, they come for the eggs. Just another unearned treat for the New World Vulture. I've read that herons, much like the vultures, have their own clade where they gather and commingle after a long day. But I doubt it's as disgusting as the vulture's chortling blood howl clade I witnessed with my father in the mountains above the Flats in Dover.

Fucking vultures.

As the heron walked elegantly back into the brush to enjoy its meal, I noticed that in the water below there were hundreds of translucent jellyfish. They appeared lifeless and stuck in the slack tide, like an abundant midden of plastic bags; the kind one sees everywhere in the harbors and wetlands of Los Angeles. It took a minute for my eyes to adjust. But the longer I stood there, the more it became apparent that contrary to the jellyfishes' normal state of powerlessness—the complete inability to control their own destiny, the ebb and flow tides governing their gelatinous, weightless disposition—they were, in their own way, actually swimming, enjoying their moment in-between; that is to say, before the slack tide took its inevitable and controlling turn.

I thought of Donny. I was relieved that things blew up in Detroit. He just couldn't let it go. Pushed and pushed. Pointed out the obvious inconsistencies, so much so that violence became the only emotional recourse the kid, Joey, had left. No more tools in the bag. He was too young. Donny was offended that the kid thought he was a roadie and that he didn't care one bit about The In Between. But why should he? We wouldn't have, not when we were his age. That said, had Donny not engaged we most likely would have gone to The Old Miami, and he would have been ceaseless in his efforts of getting the original In Between back together and onto the stage. And having Rich there, were he into it (I suspected he was), it would have been hard to hold out. With Joy not feeling well and relegated to the bus, I would have been stuck either walking the streets of Downtown Detroit or going to the show. Neither seemed appealing. What appears to be sabotage for one, is actually a blessing for another.

You're impossible like that, Lord.

I walked further across the bridge to the amphitheater. The last three wooden slats connecting the bridge to the stage were missing. I jumped onto the stage; the sudden strength in my legs surprised me. The morning air, the negative ions, whatever it was, I felt good, empowered, had the whole place to myself. The venue itself was nothing more than a shed on water, a glorified mooring made of concrete that, much like the jellyfish, floated up and down with the tide. Judging from the lack of water marks, it was peak high tide.

I walked out onto the stage, front and center—artists of the highest stature had performed here—and looked out over the orchestra section; it was covered in trash, ripped out faded red plastic chair seats; plastic bottles of water and bleach; plastic bottles of detergent; plastic orange syringe caps; plastic and plastic and plastic; used aluminum cans of spray paint; discarded and dirty clothes damp from the early morning dew; human feces; bags of fast food; graffiti everywhere, so much so that the art was nonexistent. Everyone was shitting on everyone and everything. Even in art, and its inherent pretense of non-competitiveness. False. Strange how the need to be top dog, top bitch, top whatever the word-du-jour, finds its way into every corner and crevice; how the oppressed become the oppressor. What would they do without each other, with nothing to rail against? What would they do if they found out they were one in the same? Right and left, black and white.

No difference.

I looked up into the stands. *Bet ya Mick Jagger stood here, Lord.* Fucking Mick Jagger. Right here, "Paint it Black." Right here, "Jumping Jack Flash." God bless that motherfucker. What a gift. I moved my shoulders a little, closed my eyes and pushed out my lips, let my feet glide side-to-side, snapped my fingers, "Watch it!" jerked my neck and shook my hips, put my wrists on the small of my back, bent my torso, did the chicken. A toast to the man. His very existence the essence of what it means to be punk rock. All the factoids, all the journalists and their revisionist history, their paywalls and subscriptions to sell, always give the androgynous punk glory to Iggy and Lou and Bowie. Jagger came first!

Know that's right.

Like a crossfire hurricane.

"You Jimmy?" a voice said from behind me. It startled me. I turned quickly. A young, slight man wearing hippie-era John Lennon granny glasses, a loose-fitting tracksuit, approached from backstage. "I'm Arnie. We talked on the phone." He drew closer. "Looking pretty good on that stage. Rich said you were in a band. Ever play here before?"

"No… no. I thought we said 9 am."

He took in the scars on my face and motioned to the endless grot scattered over the orchestra section. "We did. I apologize for all this. We had a few encampments pop up. Tell ya man, it's like whack-a-mole with those things. But I talked with Joy this morning; wired her the $300k. Everything is—"

"$300k?" I blurted out.

"Yeah. Show must go on. We'll get it cleaned up."

To backtrack, pretend I wasn't fazed by the number *($300k*!), I quickly pulled out my cell phone. "Why didn't you call me about all this?"

He shrugged. “I did.”

“I don’t see a call.”

“It’s all good. Joy said to leave it as is.”

“Leave it as is? She hasn’t even seen the place.”

“I sent her pictures.”

“So, everyone’s going to just stand in the shit—that it?”

“No, no. We’ll… we’ll close off the orchestra, leave it as is. But the mezzanine, the food and merch and all that, that’ll all be cleaned up, that’ll be where the people are anyways. Won’t take long either. It’s really just this orchestra section that’s fucked up.”

I shook my head in disbelief, looked up into the stands.

“Hey, I hear you. Joy said she showed the pictures to Rich though, and that’s what he wants.”

I said nothing. $300k for speaking to a bunch of rich people over a pile of shit? Talk about bold. Jesus. But the more I thought about it, the more it made sense. Why cover up? Let big money see where it’s really at, give them the feeling of having been there, so much so that when they write the checks, they can tell their other big money check writing friends what’s really going on. It was old school theatrics. Brechtian.

I guess for $300k, it fucking better be.

“So, do you want to do the walkthrough now or…?”

“Sure.”

I pointed to the rusted floor monitors. “Those things work?”

“Oh yeah. Everything works. Those overheads,” he pointed above, “may not look like much, but they still pump. All he has to do is plug in the mic. It’s kind of the nice thing about Rich’s brand, low overhead.”

“What about security?”

"Put a couple people at the bridge, half dozen in the pit."

"No one's going to be in the pit now though, right?"

"That's true. We can ask Rich if he still wants them, given the conditions. If not, we'll put them over at the first rail. Honestly, with this show, security won't be an issue."

"Let's walk over to the box office. I want to see what the entrance looks like, see if we need any signage. Do you have staff that can help with a separate entrance for the meet-and-greet?"

"I think Joy wants to handle that."

"The meet-and-greet? I handle that."

"That's what she said. You can ask her though. She'll be here in a minute."

I felt a pang in my stomach. I looked across the marsh to where the bus was parked and saw Joy in her high heels and white Turley Tencel suit awkwardly walking to the bridge.

Jesus, Lord. What is she doing?

"Joy! We're over here," Arnie yelled.

"Hi, Arnie," she yelled back. "Be right there!" With her head down and looking at her feet so as to not get the high heels stuck in between the wooden slats, she held onto the guardrails and slowly walked across the bridge.

To greet her, Arnie and I walked to the edge of the stage near the bridge. Joy stopped at the three missing slats. Her hair was tousled and barely pinned together. She did not appear happy. Clearly whatever bug she caught before Detroit was still with her. "I don't think I can make this jump. Is there another way?"

"You can do it," I said, moving closer to the edge of the stage. In the water below the three missing slats, jellyfish contracted their bell-shaped bodies en masse, creating small vortex rings. "Just take off the heels, toss them."

"You know how much these things cost?"

"Toss them to me is what I mean; one at a time. I'll catch them."

"Arnie, is there no other way?"

"We can go back across the bridge. I'll drive you around to the other side, enter from there. Does that work?"

"How long will that take?"

"20-30 minutes, another 20-30 on the way back."

"This morning just keeps getting better," she said, exasperated.

"Come on, Joy. Just throw me the shoes. Take my hand and I'll help you across. Easy. It's like three feet."

She looked down at her feet, a deep breath, a resigned sigh. "Make sure you catch them." She took off her golden heels—white patent leather, Prada—and tossed them to me underhand, one at a time. I set the shoes aside then stepped even closer to the edge where the bridge connected to the stage. There was movement in the water below. The tide had turned; the jellyfish, no longer swimming, were now lost in its sway.

"You sure about this?" she asked.

Something about the way she said it, her request for reassurance, her now bare feet, plugged me in and pulled me back to a time seemingly not so long ago when we were indeed one.

I held out my hand. "On three."

"I don't know."

"Let's not do this," Arnie said. "I can—"

"Arnie!" I put my hands up as if to say, *Enough*! "Joy. I got you. You can do this." Our eyes locked. "You ready?"

She nodded, Yes.

"On three, okay? One. Two. Three." Joy grasped my left hand and leaped onto the stage. Her force nearly knocked me over. The engagement ring was loose on her finger, and the diamond dug deep into the palm of my hand. I cursed loudly, which frightened her, and tried to shake loose of her grip. But like a deer in the headlights, and still a little off-balance, she didn't let go. I again pulled my hand away from hers, and again she didn't let go. "Joy! What are you doing? Let go!" She didn't let go. The pain was excruciating. I ripped my hand away from hers. Blood trickled along the lines of my palm and dripped onto the stage.

Embarrassed by my words, I looked to Joy, then to Arnie; both appeared mortified. Reflexive and nervous, Joy wiped her hand onto both the Turley Tencel jacket and pant leg; my blood staining the white suit red. Her face turned crimson. She hung her head and let loose a deep, guttural cry of frustration and anger.

"Oh my god, oh my god. Are you okay?" Arnie said, rushing to her side and taking her hand.

"I'm so sorry about all this," she said, holding back tears, examining the damage to her suit. "Do you have anything I can clean this with, any hydrogen peroxide?"

"Of course, of course. In my office, there's a medicine cabinet. Follow me."

Arnie led us backstage through a rummage of power cables and seemingly abandoned old amp cases. A colony of feral cats wheezed and hissed and scattered about. "Used to be a lot of rats around here," Arnie said. One of the cats, a young and mangy orange tabby, followed me. Perhaps it was the blood dripping from my hand.

We entered the office; it was small and bare with a single metal desk and a couple of metal chairs. The floor was concrete, everything dark and grey.

Arnie went into the bathroom and out he came with a roll of toilet paper, a box of band aids, and a dirt smudged bottle of iodine. He set them on top of the desk. The dust was an inch thick. "Sorry, no hydrogen peroxide."

Joy closed her eyes and exhaled. She wouldn't make eye contact with me. I didn't blame her. I was angry, too. All these years later, our once immutable chemistry so far gone, we can't even complete a simple throw and catch without spectacle. *What kind of world is that, Lord*? It's embarrassing, a dishonor to what we once had. The diamond punctured a hole in the center of my palm; the blood was profuse. I grabbed the roll of toilet paper, pounded it against my pant leg to get the dust off, then dabbed at the blood. The cat, at my feet, purred and rubbed its head against my jeans.

Taking in the environs, Joy said, "This isn't where we're doing the meet-and-greet is it?"

"Yeah, this is it," Arnie said.

"We can't do a meet-and-greet here. This place is a mess."

"Oh yeah, no, you'll see. I got curtains and carpet coming, catering; got the masseuse for Rich at 3pm. This will all look one-hundred percent different. Three hours tops. Trust me."

"I don't do trust, Arnie. I'm a show me person."

"I hear that, and I'll show you. If it's not to your liking by noon, which it will be, it will, I've got a suite above the mezzanine, we can do it there."

Joy nodded. "What about security?"

"Jimmy and I were just talking about that. When we're done here, we'll go walk the grounds."

"I don't need to walk the grounds. You two can do that. What I need is a functional office."

"Already in progress. I'm on it."

She looked toward me, but not at me. "You can handle the security then?"

"Yes," I said, offended she felt the need to ask. I again dabbed the wound with the toilet paper roll. "You have a trash can or something, Arnie?"

"You can just set it there on the desk," Arnie said with antipathy. "Cleaning crew will get it."

"I'm going to need something else, Arnie."

He ignored me. "Joy, why don't we do this, there's a cleaners 15 minutes from here. They're—"

"Arnie."

"—amazing. Quick turnaround. Let's go get your suit clean."

"Yeah, let's go get that suit clean."

"Jimmy. Enough!" Joy said.

Arnie shrugged and continued, "We'll get something to eat, be back by noon. We can do the walkthrough, and if things aren't to your liking, we'll figure out a way to make you whole. We want you and Rich happy. That sound good?"

An air of hope overcame Joy's sullen face. Her enhanced and tan tattooed chest breathed in a deep sigh of relief. As if in a moment of reflection, she chuckled to herself, "Jimmy?"

"Yeah?"

"There are bandages in the bus."

***

Meet the people where they are at. Not where we want them to be. *That the way it works, Lord*? Yes. Love has nothing to do with it. Lucky I ever had any of it. Love. I again dabbed at the hole in the palm of my hand with the roll of toilet paper. The blood continued to flow as I watched Joy go back across the bridge and hop into Arnie's big black Cadillac Escalade. Something about that car, it was beautiful, and yet I hated its luxury.

I was soon overcome with a strange and delirious "I'll show her what she's missing" mentality. It was a gross kind of feeling, one that leaves the mouth tasting like astringent. I squeezed the roll of toilet paper and mashed it into the wound. At my feet, the same mangy cat sat on its rear legs and stared up at me.

"Fuck you want?" I said.

Its tail swished slowly back and forth.

"Like that, huh?"

The cat blinked, its eyes viridescent, almost emerald.

"Alright then." I set down the roll of toilet paper and with my right hand picked up the cat, its bones brittle, and cradled it into my arm. The fur wasn't actually mange, it was just wet from overgrooming. Some cats when under prolonged stress do this to self-soothe. "You a boy, a girl, what's your deal?" I asked, as it attempted to get more comfortable in my arm. "Doesn't really matter, does it? What am I going to call you?" The cat rubbed its tiny head over and over against my chest. I looked around at the debris of the backstage area; a handful of other cats, bigger, older, meaner, creeped nearby. "That your family?" The cat closed its eyes and burrowed its head deeper into my chest, away from the other cats. "I see that. Come on, let's go to the beach. I'm calling you Moses."

Rest.

***

Moses and I went to Jones Beach. The white sand wasn't really white, not like I had envisioned; it was more of a light creamy beige, just like the tuxedo I wore to Homecoming with Joy, where all we did was make out and slow dance. The sand was soft though, and the rolling dunes and beachgrass were idyllic, as were the tall, weathered lifeguard stands. The waves were not really waves, they were ripples, non-existent as far as the eye could see; very different from the waves I grew up with in Dover; more tranquil, less violent.

About one hundred yards away, I saw a woman walking in the opposite direction. Other than that, the beach was for me and Moses and a dozen or so Piping Plovers running around the small tide; a peck here, a peck there, a pause followed by a scamper, three feet to the left, three feet to the right, an attempt to trick its prey into movement and thereby become visible. A hunting dance. I once read that plovers practice courtship, literally practice it. When interested, the male will swoop high into the air then come down hard and fast onto the sand, right next to the object of its desire. Then with its chest puffed out wide, it approaches the female, cool and assured as if to say, *What ya think about that*? *You like that*? *Pretty cool, right*? A moment of insecurity, *Huh*? *What*? *No*? A couple more puffs of the chest, *What about this*?

I love everything about this dance. Every. Single. Thing.

In fact, I can hardly think of anything more pleasant than watching nature absolve itself from human analysis.

Moses fell fast asleep in my arm. And soon I with them. We awoke to the sound of a car door being shut. My face in the soft sand, a lifeguard stood over me; behind her was a red Jeep Wrangler. The sun was out.

"You alright?" she said, twenty-two maybe, stocky, solid, fit and tan.

I rose up onto my elbow and squinted, sand in the corner of my eye. She handed me a towel to wipe my face. "Homeless can't sleep here, sir."

I took the towel.

"I'm not homeless."

"Can't sleep here, sir."

Moses moved behind me. My mouth was dry. I wiped the sand off my cheek and looked up to the lifeguard. "What time is it?"

She reacted to the scars that were hidden beneath the sand caked on my face and took a step back. I nodded that I understood her concerns. "It's okay." I pointed toward the Amphitheatre. "I'm with the show tonight."

"There is no show tonight, sir. City is shutting it down."

"Since when?"

"Since now."

"I was just with the guy. Arnie."

"I don't know who that is, sir. But the venue's not safe. You need something for your hand?" I hadn't thought about my hand. The bloody roll of toilet paper lay next to me. "I can get you something; get you bandaged up."

I slowly sat upright. "Thank you."

The Lifeguard went to the Jeep. I turned to Moses who was now crouched, eyes intent on the darting Piping Plovers. In an instant, Moses took off and with its left paw stunned one of the birds. The bird lay still in the sand. Moses played with it, boxed it a few times. The bird did not move. Then, as if afraid someone or something would come to take its conquest away, Moses quickly looked over its shoulder, to the left and to the right. A hunter always knows when it's most vulnerable. When safety was assured, Moses gently picked up the bird with its mouth and brought it to me, laid it at my feet;

and with a clear smile sat up on its hind legs, stared into my eyes, and slow blinked.

A gift, Lord...

I was overcome.

Now what?

***

One might think I would've been quick in anger or response to Joy's "Bandages in the bus." But that's not how it works when there is history. The old wounds feel normal. Like home. Like I wouldn't even know who I was or what to do without them. So, I let the hurtful words enter my being. I feel every ounce they have to give until I go blank. I'm not proud of this, the blank thing. And I'm not saying it's the right way to process emotion. I envy people who in the moment can freely speak their mind. But that kind of thing never worked for me; get your ass handed to you by doing shit like that. I learned that early and often.

The older I got, the more normalized it became. Even in recovery, all these years later, I would find another way to justify doing the same thing; namely, take the punch, for to say something in the moment that I am later going to regret, something hurtful that I cannot take back, seems worse than taking the initial blow. End up having to take two punches. Then, if you want to be sane, you have to make amends, have to be human. Ugh.

Nothing worse than that.

Of course there is a selfish component to it all: Nikad im daj zadovoljstvo da znaju da mogu da te povrede. Nikad. *Never give them the satisfaction of knowing they can hurt you. Never.* Is this healthy? No. Would I recommend it to an enemy? No.

Do I again contradict myself?
Jebi se! *Fuck you*!
My way.

The drive home to Dover was long and arduous, more than I ever would have imagined. I caught the flu bug that Joy had, as did Rich, and for two full days sweated it out in my tiny coffin of a bunk, rolling to the left and to the right as Donny seemingly sped his way through every scenic route and mountain pass. With Moses at my side, I dipped in and out of consciousness, reality blurred by a repetitive fever dream that blended bits and pieces, fragments of reality: a bully from middle school with his random fiend of a friend who with no restraints held me captive in some small, dank and darkened room, taunting me as I swung my fists at their teenage faces. I swung and I swung and I swung and, still, nothing happened, no blows would land. I had no power to escape, to fight back against whatever it was they wanted to do to me.

At one point I got up to use the restroom, and I do mean use the restroom, which is no-go on a tour bus. It was either there or in the bunk. Inside the restroom was a small captain's window. We were in the mountains somewhere, the Poconos I imagined, though we could've been anywhere, and it was magnificent, majestic; an exalted ghost, a white mist sunrise soaring in and through the tall and heroic green pine. It was perhaps the most beautiful thing I had ever seen and yet I shook so violently I thought I might die right there on the toilet just like Elvis.

They did him dirty. He deserved better!

On the third day, late afternoon, the fever broke, and my appetite somewhat returned. Moses had left the bunk. My hand was still wrapped tightly in a gauze bandage the lifeguard had given me. My clothes wet from fever, I changed into a pair of black Turley sweats then went and rummaged the small refrigerator for food. There was nothing but scraps, leftover sandwich meat, picked at-celery and carrots, handful of grapes, some unwrapped and stale bread. I grabbed a Gatorade, and a bottle of water then went and sat upfront with Donny. Moses lay licking himself in the passenger seat.

"Ahhh, sleeping beauty awakes," Donny said.

I set the Gatorade and water down and picked up Moses; his entire coat was wet.

"Dude, that cat's been licking itself forever."

"It's a nervous thing," I said.

"Pretty fucking nervous," he said. "You look like Rich in those sweats. How ya feeling?"

"I'm alright. What are you listening to?"

"*Bolero*. Been listening to it since North Dakota."

"Why are we in North Dakota?"

"We're not. We're in Montana."

"Okay… why are we in Montana?"

"Rich wanted a vacay. Took 'em to an Airbnb."

"Are they not in the bus?"

"I just told you they're at an Airbnb."

"What are we supposed to do?"

"We're supposed to go to Wal-Mart and get food."

"Wal-Mart?"

He turned up the music. "Don't fuck up my flow, bro. Listen to that. It's insane. The swirls and movement, those march rolls with no contrast, all of it, each bit, it's like he's just saying, 'This is what I am. This is what I do.' You think he knew it would be his last piece, like, subconsciously or some shit?"

"Ravel? For sure."

"Fucking brilliant! Helluva way to go out. Helluva way." He closed his eyes and raised his arm, his wrist rotating up and down, left and right, anticipating each movement as if he were the conductor. "Wonder who that drummer is, what their life's like? Should've gone that route."

"Still can."

"Please."

"You don't know what's in store. Stay clean, do anything you want with music. Write your own symphony."

"Yeah, shit… those fuckers, living real lives. Probably all have nice little flats, girlfriends and boyfriends, whatever. Keep their shit nice and tight, instruments all shined up. Show up on time. Play some sick place, crazy old concert hall with insane acoustics. That's just for rehearsal! I mean, fuck, that's living. That's real living."

"Starting to sound sober." I rolled down the window for some air; it was refreshing, cool. We were on a straightaway, a two-lane highway in a verdant basin of tall grass and sizable cattle bordered by extinct volcanic mountain ranges. Cold from the wind, Moses twitched and burrowed deeper into my lap. I rolled up the window. "Have you slept?"

"No, fuck no. Do need to take a shit though, before those clouds roll in. See that? That's hell dark. Coming in quick, too." He looked me in the eye. "Speaking of taking a shit, Dude, you took a shit in the bathroom?"

"Just watch the road."

"I can't believe you did that. I mean, everyone knows you don't take a shit on the bus. I don't even know what to say, destroyed the whole cabin ya nasty fuck." He laughed and offered a big smile, turned his attention back to the road. "Gotta show some respect, bro. I mean, we're not savages."

"That's debatable."

"Dude, you really do look like Rich in those sweats."

"Anything else you want to comment on?"

"Yeah, actually; been talking to myself for days."

"So, is he putting us up or what are we doing?"

"Man, I don't know, and I don't really care; just nice to be out on the road."

Bolero on high, filling every nook and corner of the cabin, we exited the highway. The clouds were low and leaden, a sound of thunder in the distance like some kind of nuclear boom. Donny turned off the music. A hard rain began to fall. We drove up slowly to the offramp stop sign. In a pastoral patch of small grass, a family of vultures pecked at the carcass of a recumbent and gargantuan cow. One of the vultures perched itself stolid high above the others on top of the cow's ribcage. The overseer.

I again rolled down the window.

"The fuck you doing? It's freezing," Donny said.

The rain came in sideways and pelted my face. Moses leapt off my lap. Compelled, I reached into the glove compartment and grabbed the owner's manual to shield the rain and better my view. The overseer stood three feet tall and towered above the other vultures who, in an orgy of blood, savagely pecked at the cow's innards.

The cow blinked.

"Sacred cow," I said under my breath.

"What?"

"Listen."

We came to a full stop.

The cow moaned.

"Oh, fuck dude, that thing's alive?"

"It's a sacred cow."

"That's disgusting. Come on, man, close the window."

"No, this is a thing; it's giving itself. Stay here."

The overseer turned toward the bus, its crop, thick and elongated, bore the shape of an 'S'. We made eye contact. Instinctively, I leaned back to protect myself.

"Oh, fuck dude, that thing's an animal. Roll that shit up, man."

Distracted, Donny let his foot off the brake then quickly stepped back onto the brake. No seatbelt, I fell forward, my bandaged hand hard into the dash. I yelled out and looked to the overseer. It waddled in place side-to-side, 3X as if a dance, then ever so slightly puffed its chest and revealed its New World white-tuft identity. The rain turned violent; it bounced five feet up off the concrete. Windshield wipers were of no use, like trying a wash a river.

"Close the fucking window!"

I again closed the window. As I did, the overseer grunted and hissed; its black silhouette on top of the sacred cow grew faint through the grey blue rain pounding the windshield.

***

We pulled into an empty Wal-Mart parking lot; a few cars here and there, but that was about it. The rain still fierce, Donny and I exited the bus and made a run for the entrance. We were greeted by an armed security guard: stocky, fifty pounds overweight, most of it in the barrel of her belly and chest. There was an inward curve at her ribs so pronounced it appeared they had been removed with a hatchet. She chewed on a plastic toothpick and wore a makeshift eye patch made with a heap of gauze bandage. Scotch tape sprawled in all directions across the bridge of her nose, forehead, and cheeks. With her one eye, she sized us up, a judgmental once over, then nodded in the direction of the restrooms.

"What I'm talking about," Donny said to me. "Meet ya back here?"

"I'm going to go look around."

"Did you bring your cell?"

No.

"I'll never find you in this place. Just wait here. Trust me… shit won't be long. Get it, shit won't be long."

I looked to the security guard. She lifted her upper lip, a thin unkempt wiry mustache, then rotated the toothpick to the other side of her mouth. "Can keep me company if ya like."

My stomach burned with a groan of obligation; the kind you learn as a small child but can never really shake: Be hospitable even if it kills you. I could see Donny's enormous smile through the back of his head (clearly knowing my glaring defect) as he walked away.

"Don't tell me," the guard said. "California."

I nodded, Yes.

"Whereabouts?"

"Los Angeles, mostly."

"Too bad."

"Why, where are you from?"

"Bakersfield."

"Home of Buck Owens."

"Got that right."

"Bakersfield sound."

She seemed pleased and nodded to a set of white plastic chairs against the wall. "Sit in one of those if you want." She patted the badge. "No funny business though."

"That's okay, been sitting too long. What's the badge?"

"You don't wanna find out. What do you know about Buck Owens and Bakersfield, anyways? Don't look like you got any country in ya."

"I know who the Buckaroos are, played Carnegie Hall. Kind of a big deal for country folk, wouldn't you agree?"

She bit her lower lip and tapped her .45 at her belt. "You probably Googled it."

That brought a smile to my face. I probably should not have been so snarky, but some people don't respect respect; they respect and expect a struggle. A recognition of power. Who's the top?

"What's your name?" I asked.

"What, California can't read?" She lowered her chin to the nameplate on her chest. *Connie Wilson.*

"Connie, my name is Jimmy."

"What happened to your face, Jimmy?"

That's how it starts isn't it, Lord?

"A student stabbed me."

"Student. You a teacher?"

"Something like that."

"'Bout your friend, what's his name? Seems sketchy."

"Donny. He's alright. Great musician. Really great. He knows all about that Bakersfield sound; big into Haggard."

"Haggard's a criminal." With exaggeration, she lifted her arm and checked her watch. "I gotta go make rounds. You get hungry, there's a food court on the other side."

With a slight limp, her left leg considerably shorter than her right, she waddled away.

Not an easy name. Connie.

What happened in Bakersfield?

Why here, why this: the gun, the limp, the toothpick? The caved in ribs.

The more I thought about it, why not here?

Why not this? Why not the gun?

Bandages in the bus.

***

Donny came back bright eyed and antsy. "Dude, I'm fucking starving. There's a McDonalds over there. Let's go." We walked for what seemed like a purblind mile of polished concrete. The fluorescent lights above were oppressive, so I kept my head low to avoid triggering a migraine. There were twenty or thirty, maybe forty, checkout counters but only three cashiers, each of them white with their gawks and stares, neck bows and head turns, whispers, mostly directed at Donny. It was like they had never seen a Black man in person, let alone one whose essence screamed, *I'm him*!

The refulgent red and yellow lights of the McDonald's golden arches were magnetic, if illusory, and the smell of chemicals and oil and bread and processed sugar and processed salt and french fries and whatever kind of processed meat they were slinging made my mind ill and my stomach starved. There were no employees to take our order; the store was fully automated. We punched a code into a screen and within seconds a soda fountain to our left filled the drinks—a Cherry Coke for Donny, and a regular Coke for me—and from a lift out came two trays filled with food.

We went into an adjacent room to sit down and eat. There were a dozen or so tables, again with the blinding fluorescent lights above. The room was enclosed and relatively empty except for an elderly mustached man with an indigo-blue down jacket and a well-worn straw Stetson hat. He sat near the entrance, his eyes silver, and face lined with the book of years. On the table next to his tray lay an old-style pistol with a mahogany grip; it was polished, black as night.

In the back of the room, up against the wall sat a sizable family of four: wedding rings; the husband was big and tall, thick around the midsection with a beard, trucker hat, a real one, and a cold million mile stare; the wife was soft and plump, sad if content with blue eyes, overwhelmed, perhaps, by her husband's time on the road, their two young girls, five or six, maybe seven, fighting over a pile of french fries. The husband leaned his back against the wall and put a protective arm around his wife, gently tapped her shoulder. She looked to me and then to Donny and promptly shushed the kids.

Distracted by their fear, I bumped into a nervous eyed man and his cigarette smoking wife who were leaving the room. I nearly spilled my tray of food and quickly apologized. The man bowed his hatted head and raised his eyebrows as if to say, *What's this world coming to*? Their trays were still filled with food.

Donny chose to sit down at the exiting couple's table. A single french fry, a scattering of salt. The yellow plastic booth seats still warm.

"Dude, they smoke cigarettes here. How cool is that? I should start smoking again." He flicked a leftover french fry off the table then quickly unwrapped his double Big Mac and took a monster bite. The special orange sauce dripped down onto his scraggled, kinky, salt and pepper beard. "You know what, man? Gotta say it, these motherfuckers, McDonald's, they deserve to still be around. I mean, this thing, this fucking Big Mac, pound for pound, probably best burger there is."

"Best burger? Please."

"No, I'm serious. All those fancy fifty-dollar burgers, ain't got nothing on this."

With my unbandaged hand, I unwrapped the Quarter Pounder—it had been years since I'd had one—and took a small bite; lukewarm, the cheese, unmelted. I set the burger down and made short-lived eye contact with the man with the gun.

Donny slurped his Cherry Coke and took another massive bite of his Big Mac. "No good?"

"It's cold."

He raised his hand and flittered it about like I was stupid. "If you go with the Quarter Pounder you gotta go double, otherwise they give you the old shit. Send it back."

"You see that guy with the gun?"

He smirked. "Eh. Personally, I'm for it; keeps shit tight. Should have it in L.A., might stop some fools from fucking around."

I dipped into some of the french fries. "Where you eating fifty-dollar burgers, anyways?"

"I lived in Venice. We invented that shit."

"Whose we? What, you're from Venice now?"

"Ghost town, baby. Since '91." He stuffed the last bite of the Big Mac into his mouth. "I should've gotten two. I'm telling ya, man, this burger… outlast all those chichi L.A. places."

"Yeah, okay."

"Wanna know why?"

"I already know why. Chemicals."

"Chemicals?"

"The whole thing, it's a chemical."

"No, no, no, no, no. You're missing the point. It will outlast them because it's good, and it's cheap."

"You just paid twenty-two bucks for that thing."

"That's only 'cause I got the Double Mac and the Double Fries. Still cheaper."

"Yeah, it's cheap all right."

"Hey, keeps people loyal. You should take note of that."

"What?"

"Keep the street, you survive. You lost the street."

"Being cheap is not loyalty, it's gimmickry. It's how they keep the kids hooked."

"Ahhh, fuck the kids, man," his voice raised. "Come on. Everything's about the fucking kids nowadays. Kids. Kids. Kids. Kids. All gonna die. Shit. They gonna die too. Better to go out keeping it real at Mickey D's than some white ass linen place. Why does everything have to be white anyways? Should be black linen. Look better."

"It would look better."

"Right? Some bamboo chairs. Purple napkins."

"I don't know about purple."

He filled his fingers full of fries and shoved them in his mouth, sucked the salt and oil from his thumb. "And I'll tell ya, those fancies, all the duck fat and shit they flavor the meat with, bet their burgers got more saturated fat than a fucking Big Mac."

"Donny, you got to wipe your beard, man; got orange sauce all over it."

He laughed and with a napkin dabbed at his beard making it worse. "And at least McDonald's ain't lying about it."

"This place lies every day, all day. It's what they do."

"No. Uh uh. Those other places, they're the ones lying. Try to make you feel like you did something good for yourself, call it healthy fats and shit, like it's good for your brain. It's bullshit. McDonald's don't say healthy fats."

"So, it's a 'you lie, we all lie' logic?"

"You do it."

"Do what?"

"Lie."

"Okay."

"No?" His voice raised another notch. "You. Jimmy Marsan, don't like to point out where all the hypocrisy is, that's not you, that what you're telling me?" He pounded his hands as if a thunderous drum roll onto the table.

I looked to the man with the gun. He nodded his head slow one time, his steely stare now unapologetic and fixed on both me and Donny.

"Can you just clean your beard? Making me claustrophobic."

"Truth is making you claustrophobic, bro."

"Whole place is making me claustrophobic. Let's just go."

"Fuck that. Gotta finish my fries first. See, I got it all figured out, what your deal is. Took me a minute but… now that I'm clean," he stuffed more fries into his mouth, "I can see it. Pretty simple, too. You spot it, you got it."

I paused. Something about his eyes, he looked different, mean and vindictive. "Where are you going with this; what are you doing?"

He shook his head from side-to-side, as if I should have known. "What I'm doing is," he pointed down, "saving your ass," then pointed to my face, "from your ass."

"Saving me?" I said aloud. "You, saving me?"

"Logic is what got your ass here, am I right?"

"What? What the fuck are you talking about?"

"Logic, fucker, logic!"

"Hey! Language," the large man with the family said. My face flushed with embarrassment. I turned to apologize but before I could say anything the man, eyes expressive, agitated, continued. "Trying to have a peaceful dinner. Okay?" He nodded to his wife and small children. "Get it right. Do better."

"We'll keep it down. I'm sorry."

The man appeared offended by the apology.

"Yeah, Jimmy. Keep it down," Donny said loudly.

I lowered my voice. "Let's just go. Place has bad energy."

"Eh, what's he gonna do? Besides, I got shit I gotta say, and I don't want to say it on the bus. Joy says—"

"Joy says?"

"You gonna let me talk or you gonna keep interrupting? Joy says, I've been stuffing my feelings too long; that's what's keeping me strung out. So…"

"So, express your feelings then."

"I'm worried about you. There, I said it."

"Worried about me?"

"Yeah."

"Should be worried about yourself."

"Nah, that's the problem. You're not listening. You been living up in the head too long; logic, it's bad man, unhealthy; that little perch of academia. You wanna know what unhealthy is, that shit's unhealthy."

"What is this, an intervention?"

"Kind of."

"It's my job. I'm a teacher. I teach."

"Job? It's not your job motherfucker. You don't have a job. Look at you. Act like you're above everybody, like you know everything, but you don't, you're all fucked up; just a bunch of fancy words on the EBT… no difference. What do they say? No earthly good."

"No earthly good?"

"You heard me," he said, louder. "No. Earthly. Good."

I took a hard shallow breath, pared my eyes to quell the rising anger and disbelief. "This from the man in rehab."

He shrugged.

"The one I took him to, who thirty-something days ago lived in a Chinook; not in Venice, the 90291, an alley of trash, hypodermic trash behind the AMF, in a Chinook—my

Chinook." He rolled his eyes, gestured inward with his hands as if to say, *Keep it coming*. "Asking for a sober coach, remember? Remember that? For Punk Fest seventy thousand, wants to make amends and pay me back but doesn't pay me back, leaves me in the park with the Lil Cycos to go get strung out with some rando."

"Rosie's not a *rando*."

"No, she's dead. All this time you said nothing. And I'm No earthly good?" He glared and laughed out of his nose as one does when they decide what they've heard is beneath a response. *He wasn't wrong was he, Lord*? No. No, he wasn't. But I continued. "You always want to know why I won't do The In Between, why we're not together. It's this shit. It's you. It's always you. Circles. Junky ass punk rock blaze of glory circle of bullshit. That's not punk rock, Donny. Not even close. Punk rock's mowing the lawn. It's doing the hard stuff that everyone's too fat and lazy to do. And you know it. Just circles, hamsters on a wheel, all you fucks, telling the same old stories."

He growled aloud. "Noooooohhh! We're not together because you think you're not in the circle! But *you are* in the circle, bro. You are in the circle. And everyone knows it but you. Rich knows it. Joy knows it. Joy for damn sure knows it. They feel sorry for you, bro. Like you're some kind of fucking charity case or something. But not me. I know who you are. Shit," he pointed and waved his hands chaotically toward my chest, "whatever this is. Is bullshit. You think 'cause you ain't on the wheel you're above it. But you're not. You're out of the game. We're all here, boots on the ground."

"Boots?"

"Living. Working. Getting after it. What are you fucking doing? Playing mental hopscotch with the fucking fuck fuck's, the establishment, the ones who ain't ever gonna give you nothing. Shit. Left your band, left your mom—"

"What?!"

"Someone had to say it."

"Leave my mom out of this, Donny. Right fucking now."

"Just go see her, then. Not complicated. It's your fucking mom. *Family*!"

"Okay then!" the man with the gun said firm, loud. "That'll be enough." He tapped his gun 3X on the table and stood up.

"We're just talking old-timer. Take it easy," Donny said.

"Yeah, I'm just talking too," the man said. Gun in hand, he walked to the edge of our table. He was skinny and frail and stood in between me and Donny. "Time for you go now."

"I ain't going anywhere," Donny said.

"I'm sorry, sir. You're right. We're leaving. Come on, Donny. Let's go."

"I ain't done with my fries."

"You've been asked politely," the man said. "Time to go."

"Said I ain't done with my fries." Donny deadpanned the man and stuffed more fries into his mouth.

Connie entered the room, a perverse knowing grin underneath her mustache. She walked casual and confident to our table. "Problems here, Stud?"

He kept his hard, aged eyes fixed on Donny. "Nooo, I don't think so. They're just leaving."

"Stud? That's a weird name," Donny said under his breath.

"You can call him Sir," Connie said.

The large man with the family came to the table and stood behind me, just enough for me to sense his presence. "Need any help here?"

I grew uncomfortable and quickly stood up from the table. The large man put me into a rear chokehold. His arms were fat and thick; the strength of his grip intense, like that of a python. I raised my hands to give up but could not speak. He had complete control. My adrenaline surged. I writhed and wrenched but could not break free. I could barely breathe.

"What you wanna do, Stud?" the large man said.

"Oh, I don't know. I think these boys just forgot where they were."

Donny grabbed the gun from Stud.

"I ain't forget shit, *Stud*."

Connie quickly reached for her gun and yelled, "K-K-K… kee… kee… keep, keep your hands where I can see them!" In her haste and fear she lost balance and fell backwards knocking over a table and some chairs on her way down to the black and white linoleum floor.

Donny pointed the gun at Connie then back to Stud. "Uh, uh. No. You too, old-timer. Hands up."

The old man put his hands up.

Donny looked to me confidently and nodded his head: I got this.

"Let him go," Donny said to the large man. The large man squeezed my neck tighter. Donny waved the gun. "Ain't my first rodeo, bro. Let him go."

The large man did not let go. I tried to use my elbows to break free, but his hold was too strong, his stomach too large. I had no leverage. I made eye contact with Donny, shook my head, No! Don't do this. His face fell flat, as if I had again let him down. The gun went limp in his hand. He turned his eyes down and away, a look of contempt and reflection, as though all the years of our relationship crossed his mind. He glanced to Connie, and motioned both hands upward as if to say, *It's cool. I'll put the gun down*. Only he didn't say that, and the gun in his flaccid hand was moving as Connie shot him in the thigh, the stomach, and the head. He fell onto the black and white linoleum floor; his legs twisted like a pretzel. I howled and roared and scorched my constricted throat, used my legs to stomp and kick and get my way out of the chokehold. The large man was too strong. He slammed me down onto the floor, my face a few inches from Donny's; his eyes open, upward, gone, in an expanding pool of blood. The gun lay next to his head. The old man picked up the gun. Blood dripped from the handle onto the floor. Connie stood up and yelled, "He was gonna shoot me! He was gonna shoot me!" The large man put his knee into my neck. I gasped for air. "Come cuff this guy, Connie! I can't hold him forever like this!" Connie stepped over Donny's body and grabbed my arms. "He was gonna shoot me! You see that, Stud? You see that?"

"Yeah, I saw it."

"He was gonna shoot me for sure!"

Connie handcuffed me. The large man smacked me in the back of the head. Donny's pool of blood reached my face and touched my lips, a taste of salt and metal. I began to hyperventilate, spurting and spitting Donny's blood away from my face.

"Okay, okay," the old man said. "Let's get him up."

The large man lifted me off the floor. I was delirious and, still gasping for air, moaned and wailed and kicked and stomped and used my weight to get him off balance. It didn't work. The man's wife and children cooly came to his side, seemingly not a care in the world. "Baby, you okay?" the wife said.

"Oh yeah, I'm okay."

"That the bad man, Daddy?" the daughter said.

"Sure is, honey."

"Glad you caught the bad man, Daddy," the other daughter said.

"I did, baby. Got him just for you. Why don't you go on with your mom now. Go get one of those Army Barbies you wanted."

"I want the one with the gun, Daddy."

"They don't have a gun, stupid," the other daughter said.

"Yes, they do."

"No, they don't."

"Yes, they do."

"No, they don't."

"Yes, they do."

"No, they don't."

"Honey," the large man said to his wife.

The wife lovingly grinned and led the bickering daughters out of the room. The large man threw me into the booth I had sat in with Donny. He grabbed my hair and pulled my head back. My neck contorted, the fluorescent lights above were a blur of white, of space and time. Raving and irrational, I groaned and spat upward at the large man's face.

"I don't know, Stud," he said calmly. "Maybe I better put him out."

"Yeah… maybe."

Rest.

***

In a long black Audi sedan, a dark winter's night dream, I drive through a forest in Germany. An orange bottle of pills lay sexy underneath the lights of the dash. My name is on them. Dilaudid. High as fuck, mouth parched, I exit the Autobahn into a deadened forest. I get out of the car. There is a dark trail. It's raining. The trees are deciduous, tall and grey and jagged. The only light is that of the Audi, still running. A strong wind blows. The car lights turn off. I follow the trail; broken branches are everywhere. The rain whips my eyes, and my feet submerge into the soggy leaves. I come to a steep, almost vertical drop, then slide down a thin and narrow circular trail filled with mud, rock, and thick tree branches. There is plastic everywhere, bags, bottles, containers. I can't feel anything. Nothing. Not one thing. I'm still sliding. Two shooting stars of different colors whizz directly above my head, one after the other. The slide stops, and I am thrust out onto grey cobbled concrete. There has been some kind of disaster. Wooden fences, trellises with pink flowers are scattered about. Soaked petals, pounded, deluged by rain, lay over the concrete. I am afraid and desperate to find my vehicle. I look up to find the trail but it's not there and I realize how far I have fallen. I check my pocket to see if I still have the keys to the car. I do. I am surprised that when falling they did not cut me. Not even one scratch. Why? It's morning now. Morning. I consider how to trek back to the car. There's a shortcut. Very clearly, I can see it. Laying in the rubble there are signposts, a bunch of them; torn in two, rusted nails beaten into wooden stakes. They all say the same thing: Caution Snakes. I see a snake slithering near my feet, but it doesn't strike; it doesn't do anything. I walk through the signposts into an arch made of stone. Suddenly, I realize how afraid I am of snakes. My heart races and I run back through the stone arch only to see another route to the car. I now recognize where I am; it's the street I grew up on in Dover. Something has happened. There is yellow police tape all around. Everywhere: DO NOT CROSS. Two monkeys appear; their faces human, caricatures of people I know yet don't know. They are laughing at me. I start walking, and they follow.

I don't know where I'm going.

***

Lying on my back, I awoke to the sound of a baseball bat beating on a metal trash can. Above me, three fluorescent lights were suspended on a pull chain; around me, dozens of cylindrical bars, white, plastic—three inches thick, three inches apart—and at least twenty feet high with no apparent ceiling; nothing above but fluorescence and darkness. I gradually moved my fingers, my hands and arms. The floor beneath me was cold and concrete, polished with a suffocating scent of disinfectant.

"Oh good, sleeping beauty's awake," Connie said. She flung the trash can onto the floor; it clanked and clanged as my eyes in search of consciousness spun in the back of my head. All I could see through the white bars was her looming figure. I looked for Donny.

He wasn't there.

He wasn't there, Lord.

He wasn't fucking there!

Like an animal, I growled and groaned and stuck my arm in between the plastic bars, viciously grabbing at Connie's pantleg and pawing at her boots. She jabbed my wounded hand with her baton. I screamed and attempted to recoil but my elbow got stuck in between the bars. She grunted and again struck my hand with the baton and with her boot stomped on my wrist. I writhed and contorted and yelled aloud. My elbow slipped back through the bars. I rolled myself into a corner of the white plastic cage and looked for a way out. The cylindrical bars offered no way to climb, nothing to hold onto. I looked back to Connie with rage and disgust. Her bent figure lightly swayed in between the bars; the bandaged eye appeared and disappeared. All I could hear was the sound of the metal keys hanging from her belt tapping the plastic as if she were thrusting her pelvis into the bars.

One, two, three.

One, two, three.

One, two, three.

She flung Rich's little green book, *I AM: The New Rich*, inside the cage. It landed at my feet. "Friends in high places, huh? Lucky you."

I slowly opened the book to the dedication page:

For Joy,

My life, my love…

"They'll be here in a minute, Mr. and Mrs. Turley."

The back hand of God. *Good one, Lord. Congratulations.*

I laughed and looked away.

One, two, three.

One, two, three.

One, two, three.

"What's so funny?" she asked.

I thought real hard, what I was going to say next. Didn't take but a second either. An instinct, a hydroponic rush of clarity. Instead of counting, I calmly laid onto my back and stared straight into the light. Death had come for us both, Donny and me. *Only mine would not be so gentle would it, Lord*? No.

I cruelly rubbed the scars on my face.

"You want to know how I got these scars, Connie?"

"What?"

"You wanted to know how I got these scars. That's what you said."

There was silence.

"I was just… messing around," she said.

"You were just… messing around; thought it would be fun to comment on my appearance. Did I comment on your appearance, Connie?"

"You looked like trouble. And I was right!"

I continued my stare into the light.

"You were right, Connie."

"You threatening me?"

"No. That's not my thing."

"I got three witnesses. Three! That boy was gonna kill me."

"No. *He* wasn't." I stood up and walked over to the white bars she hid behind. "I am."

I AM.
I AM.
I AM.

SPECIAL THANKS

First and foremost, a special shout of love and gratitude to the CRK readers. I am overwhelmed and thankful for your enthusiastic support and interest in the work. A writer lives in a vacuum, on and on and on it goes with all sorts of internal and external debris swirling around. When (and if) we emerge from the cyclonic acropolis, we are in desperate need of fellowship and community. You are that community! The circle is complete.

Luckily, we kept the band together on this one! A heartfelt shout of gratitude to my publisher, Dan Yaryan and the good folks at Mystic Boxing Commission, for your continued belief in the work and your willingness to put CRK out and into the ether; to author, filmmaker, and captain of the ship, Ron Yungul, this book is only possible with you at the helm; to Mike Kelley, writer, artist, renaissance man, for your friendship and patient ear all these years later; to uber-talented musician and producer, Baby Burrito, for your willingness to take a break from your album and help with those final edits (wouldn't have been the same without you!); and lastly to new member of the band, author, filmmaker, and musician, Jamie Sims Coakley, for bringing your sharp and well-honed creative insight to the CRK family.

—GxC 8/28/25

About the Foreword and James Remar:

James Remar is one of my favorite actors of all time. I am entranced by the sensitivity he exudes on the screen. That he read my first novel, "California Roadkill," is an honor; that he liked it enough to write a review (see genxcore.com) and now a foreword for "California Roadkill 2: The In Between," is out-of-body, and I am most grateful.

—GenXCore

–from IMDb (October 2025):

James Remar first gained recognition in 1979 as Ajax, in the cult classic film "The Warriors." Since then he has run the gamut of roles and solid career choices: Dutch Schultz in Francis Coppola's "The Cotton Club," Albert Ganz in Walter Hill's "48 Hrs.," and Richard Wright in HBO's "Sex and the City," for which he won a SAG award.

In the sensational Showtime series, "Dexter," James played Dexter's wise and compassionate adoptive father, Harry Morgan, and was nominated for both a SAG and Emmy award. He also enjoys the distinction of being the only actor to die twice as two different characters Quentin Tarantino's "Django Unchained." He later reunited with Tarantino in the Academy Award winning "Once Upon a Time... in Hollywood;" and then in yet another Academy Award winning film, starred in Christopher Nolan's "Oppenheimer."

Currently, he is reprising his Harry Morgan character in the Paramount+ hit series "Dexter: Resurrection," as well as starring in the upcoming HBO series "Welcome to Derry," a prequel to Stephen King's "IT". Soon he'll be starring in yet another Chrisopher Nolan film, the much anticipated, "The Odyssey," an adaptation of Homer's ancient Greek poem.

About the Author

GenXCore is the author of the critically acclaimed novel *California Roadkill*. A high school dropout, he earned a Bachelor's and Master's degree in his 40s from California State University, Long Beach. He lives in Los Angeles. This is his second novel.

EXTRAORDINARY

WWW.SPARRINGARTISTS.COM

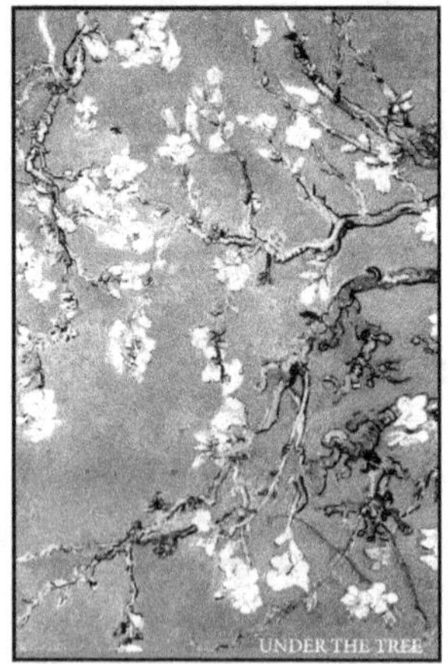

BOOKS FROM MBC!

WWW.SPARRINGARTISTS.COM

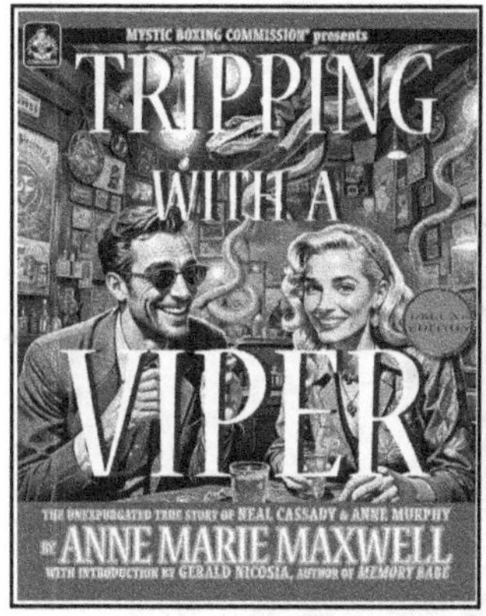

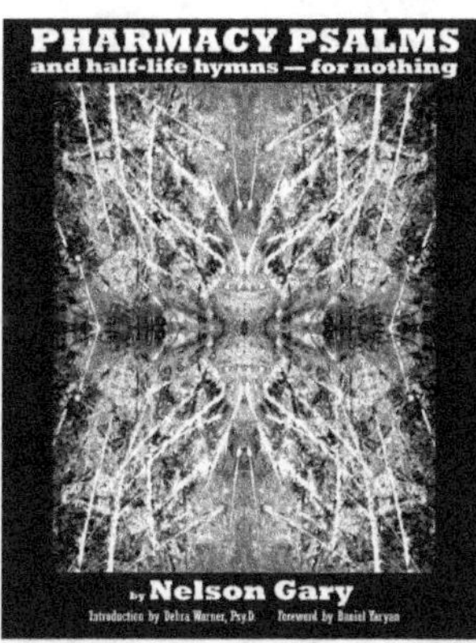

DELUXE LARGE (U.S. LETTER SIZE) BOOKS NOW AVAILABLE!

NEW DELUXE EDITIONS COMING SOON!

MBC

www.ingramcontent.com/pod-product-compliance
Lightning Source LLC
LaVergne TN
LVHW010947110826
845149LV00015B/3251

* 9 7 9 8 9 9 0 5 6 2 3 9 4 *